THE REBEL

A LEGION OF PNEUMOS NOVELLA

H.B. RENEAU

VESALIAN PUBLISHING

Mount Ánghen
ARID
Olphéis Plains
Grêgür Pass
Grêgür Gorge
Abalás
Dírol
Ulgáris
Ídarin
Western Plains
Ceffí
Crîd Eálas
Berllána
Ka
Map of Loren
240 M.E.

the North
Port
Tuálath
Port
Cála
Port
Calaén
Fertile Inlet
Eastern Plains
Port
Mârfa
Southern Shield
Tibolé

CHAPTER

ONE

"**G**et back 'ere, you good for nothin' river rat!"

The breath ripped from Neval's lungs as he ducked and wove through the market stalls. One hand clutched the loaf of bread against his side as the other tugged his hood more firmly over his head.

"You can't hide from me!"

Peeking around the corner of the fruit stand, Neval caught sight of Ewan the baker, just a few strides away. Ewan had some girth about him and his face was turning red with exertion and fury. But one glance at his corded forearms, molded by a lifetime of kneading dough, made Neval break out in a cold sweat.

Focus, he reminded himself, fixing his eyes straight ahead. *You've got this.*

Then his foot caught the lip of the fruit vendor's wagon.

The world teetered to one side, and Neval's stomach lurched into his throat. He staggered forward, barely catching himself before he dove headfirst into a stack of river plums. Oscar, the obsessive fruit vendor, had precisely arranged them into a stacked pyramid and their sickly sweet smell, already rotting in the muggy morning heat, wafted up to Neval, making his stomach roll once more. With disgust, he peeled his fingers away from the wagon's sticky surface. Ducking beneath the wagon, Neval nearly cleared it, but at the last moment cracked his head painfully against the

1

opposite lip. Pain shot through his skull and took up a pulsing beat just behind his eyes. Still, he forced himself to run on, driven purely by adrenaline and fear.

With every pounding step, he gained distance on the baker, even as the shock of impact reverberated in his ears. Still, he barreled onward, keeping to the crowded central stalls of the Ceffí village market while carefully avoiding the red-cloaked and heavily armed Bellators that patrolled the market's edge. He gasped in relief as the market stalls thinned and he could just make out the stone spire of the schoolhouse rising above the hills that cradled the sleepy upland village.

Without warning, a booted foot jutted out before him, sending Neval sprawling forward. One knee cracked painfully against the base of the village well. Staggering to his feet, Neval spun around, eyes glinting even as he tugged his hood more surely over his features. The culprit had already disappeared into the teaming crowd and Ewan stood triumphant before the fruit wagon, his towering frame dwarfed by the mountain of river plums.

"You won't get away that easy, you filthy pond scum! I'll 'ave your guts for filling!"

Heads turned their way, but Neval ignored them, smirking at the baker's arrogance. Neval was nothing if not fast. And there were very few problems he couldn't outrun when given half a chance.

It was then that the kernel of an idea tugged at his mind as his eyes shot back to Oscar's carefully crafted fruit pyramid. He scanned every inch, unconsciously calculating angles and precise trajectories. Then he saw it, a single river plum perched at an odd angle . . . perfect.

Skin buzzing with anticipation, Neval bent to scoop up a rock before he could change his mind. Its firm weight settled in his palm, and he ran a quick thumb over the smooth surface before launching it through the air.

As always, Neval's aim was perfect and the rock struck home, precisely sheering the wonky plum from its companions at the base of that flawlessly constructed pyramid. Neval caught his breath at the moment of impact. The pyramid teetered precariously, and as Ewan slowly turned, his face was a comical mix of disdain and confusion.

Then came Oscar the fruit vendor's strangled cry, quickly drowned out by the rumble of the collapsing pyramid.

Ewan tried desperately to stagger out of the way.

But before he knew it, he found himself trapped beneath the collapsing weight of the sticky fruit.

Satisfaction curled in Neval's stomach, quickly followed by alarm as other vendors turned to see what all the commotion was about.

As Oscar rushed to save his precious fruit and Ewan dug himself out from under it, Neval slipped into the teeming crowd, doubled back behind the tavern, and headed straight for the schoolhouse that lay over the far hill, its lone spire a beckoning respite.

He made it as far as the forest's edge before he had to rest.

Leaning heavily against a nearby tree trunk, Neval gasped, sucking air into his screaming lungs. He choked out a laugh of excitement and giddy relief.

Then a shadow fell over him and he froze. The voice that spoke from above was quiet, without a hint of anger or vengeance, yet filled to the brim with quiet disappointment.

"Oh, Neval, what have you done now?"

Neval swallowed hard, mind racing as he dragged himself around to face the furrowed brow of Tegan Rourke. She stood with one hand perched on her hip and the other grasping firmly onto her ever-present stack of books. Neval felt his cheeks flush crimson and he shifted his weight to either side, looking anywhere but at those soft hazel eyes that regarded him with such concern.

"Neval," she said again, her soft, lilting voice speaking in a measured cadence better suited for a horseman wrangling a spirited mare. "If you've gotten yourself into some sort of trouble . . ."

"It's nothin' Tegan, truly it — "

Her brows shot up, eyes narrowing. Tegan Rourke was a

merchant's daughter and those shrewd eyes missed nothing as they scanned his face with suspicion. Neval rolled his eyes and shot her what he hoped was a cocky grin.

"Trouble's inevitable, T, but I can always outrun it."

Her full lips twisted in a grimace as her eyes shot skyward, as if asking for patience.

"Oh yes, how could I have forgotten?" Her voice dripped with sarcasm. "Neval Brennan—he may be a thief, but at least he's a fast one."

She crossed her arms over her chest as the thick honey-colored locks she refused to braid as the other girls did fell in a curtain to one side. Yet, despite her annoyance, Tegan's face lacked the same hardness that seemed to define so many in the merchant class. Theirs was a sharpness born of fierce pride, yet tinged with fear that one misstep might send them flailing back to the gutters they'd so desperately clawed their way out of — the same gutters Neval knew all too well.

Tegan wasn't like that. She never had been. And she'd never once looked at him as anything other than a friend, no matter how different their circumstances might have been.

Neval's stomach chose that exact moment to growl traitorously, and Tegan's gaze fell to the loaf of bread in his hand. Her expression softened further.

"When did you last eat?"

Neval felt his face flush a deeper shade of red and he tensed against the pity he knew would come.

"Tell me the truth, Neval."

He swallowed tightly, ignoring the pain in his stomach.

"Saturday." He muttered, stealing a glance at her.

"That was two days ago," she said matter-of-factly, her words laced with neither surprise nor pity, for which Neval was grateful.

He gave a half shrug, ignoring the question but bouncing slightly on his feet, that familiar desire to take off running burning through his veins. But he swallowed the urge, fishing in his pocket instead for the morning's other prize. Tugging it free, he offered it toward her.

"Happy Birthday, T."

Tegan's eyes widened as they glanced from the braided silk bracelet in his hand to his face. Dropping her books, she reached out a finger to gently stroke its silky crimson length.

"It's beautiful, Neval," she breathed.

Neval inhaled sharply, feeling his insides warming rapidly at the awe in her voice, thick pleasure weaving through his veins.

"It's not—" Tegan glanced at him, eyes worried and Neval chuckled at the blush in her cheeks.

"Don't worry, I didn't steal it."

Tegan's blush deepened before her brows suddenly knit together and she yanked her hand away as if the bracelet had scalded her. Neval blinked in surprise.

"You've had this for how long, then?" Tegan demanded, hands moving back to their earlier positions planted solidly on her hips. "You haven't eaten since Saturday and you've had something this beautiful you could have traded?"

Ah, that was the problem.

Neval shrugged, kicking his bare feet intently against the dirt. When he met her eyes again, he found her usual soft, open face. But there was something else too, something sharper in her wide hazel eyes.

"Neval, I—" Her voice caught and Neval reflexively took a step toward her. So close, he could smell her floral scent, tinged as always with some expensive-smelling spice. Neval opened his mouth to reply, but suddenly found his throat inexplicably dry. He swallowed compulsively.

"Tegan—"

"There you two are!"

Tegan and Neval jumped apart, spinning in unison to see the bulky frame of Rowan Dunne. Tall and stockily built, he wore an affable grin, eyes glinting with the spark of a ready laugh. Rowan kept his sleeves rolled up to proudly display the hard-won muscle of a blacksmith's apprentice. Beside him, Neval felt like a twig, all wiry sinew and too many skipped meals. He inched another step away from Tegan.

"Now, what has you two looking so serious?" Rowan

demanded, draping an arm over each of them and pressing them against the bulk of his frame.

"Ugh, Rowan! When did you last bathe?" Neval demanded, shoving his friend away. Rowan gaped in mock indignation.

"Who *me*? I'll have you know I gave m'self a thorough dunkin' just last week!"

Neval snorted.

"Friend, I think it's time you considered increasing your frequency."

"Well, I'm hurt, Neval, just plain hurt." Rowan turned basset hound eyes to Tegan. "Are you hearin' this? My own best friend of who knows how many years? Hear how he cuts me to the core!"

With a dramatic flourish, Rowan thumped his open palm to his chest as if mortally wounded, his face stricken.

Tegan laughed, a high tinkling sound that made Neval's stomach flip.

"You too? Will you, too, mock a man when he's down?"

Tegan rolled her eyes and went to shove him away, only to shriek with laughter when Rowan pressed her closer to him, planting a playful kiss on her cheek with a loud squelching sound.

Neval felt a familiar wave of nausea as he stared resolutely away from his two best friends in the world.

"Rowan, stop! It's barely official. What'll people think?"

Neval stared at his feet, at the far-off schoolhouse, at anything and everything except the two of them. The pressure in his chest made it harder and harder to breathe.

"They'll think what a lucky bastard I am to be courtin' such a lovely creature, and newly betrothed at that!"

Betrothed.

The word sliced through Neval, through sinew and bone, until he'd swear it had pierced his very heart. For years, it had been the three of them — he and Rowan always getting into trouble and Tegan there to bail them out and clean their wounds. Rowan was like a brother to him — his opposite in so many ways, and yet perfectly complimentary. Where Rowan was strong, Neval was fast. Where Neval was clever, his brain working almost too fast for his body, Rowan was resolute, unfailing in every way.

And Tegan was . . . well Tegan was Tegan. She was their ballast, their moral compass when things fell apart. And Neval had long ago been forced to face the tragic truth that he was hopelessly, desperately in love with her.

The only problem was, she and Rowan had been courting for almost a year now.

The shift had been slow, almost imperceptible. One day, it was lingering looks, and the next it was solo outings, just the two of them, leaving Neval far behind.

"And what mishap did you get into this morning?" Rowan asked, interrupting Neval's internal misery. He nodded his head pointedly to Neval's torn pant leg, and Neval cursed silently at the sight of his bloody knee poking through. He'd have to find some way to mend it.

"Run in with Ewan," he muttered, shrugging.

Rowan snorted, shaking his head. "Third time this month. And you wonder why folk around here don't care much for you?"

Neval shot his friend a pointed look. "You know as well as I do that has nothing to do with my snatchin' a loaf here and there."

Rowan tipped his head in acknowledgement.

"You're lucky Ewan doesn't sic the Bellatorio on you," Tegan warned. "Our shop was buzzing this morning about the new centurium that arrived last night, doubling the number of Bellators in the region. Old Marta said it looks like they're building a new encampment south of the ridge."

Rowan snorted. "If there's one thing the village hates more than our fleet footed friend here . . ." He shouldered Neval affectionately at that. ". . . it's those damned Red Cloaks. I think his secret is safe, at least from them."

Neval tried to meet Rowan's grin, but knew it looked forced. He was not at all sure of that. Maybe it was time to give Ewan's bread stall a break. But how else was he supposed to eat?

"So . . . the occupation deepens. Seems like something our Crimson Quill might have some thoughts about." Rowan waggled his eyebrows playfully as he gave Tegan a proud squeeze.

"Shhh," she warned, a deep blush filling her cheeks even as her eyes darted reflexively to the castellum, the observation tower the

Bellatorio had constructed at the sound end of the village. Its stone exterior stood as a stark reminder of the Empire's power, high above the thatched roofs of their poor upland village. All the better to surveil their unwilling subjects.

Reassured there were no approaching patrols, Tegan added quietly, "The Crimson Quill may indeed have some . . . thoughts."

Rowan chuckled heartily, planting another kiss on Tegan's temple. Something heavy twisted in Neval's stomach, though not from his friends' display. As he took in the fire in Tegan's eyes as she echoed Rowan's laughter, he couldn't help the worry and dread that filled him. Did she really know what she was doing?

He quickly shoved the sensation aside. Tegan was her own person, after all. If she wanted to take such risks anonymously protesting the downlanders' occupation, who was he to stop her? Rowan certainly didn't seem worried. Why should he be?

The loud peal of a bell echoed through the town, interrupting both his friends' giggling embrace and Neval's anxiety.

"Already a quarter 'till? We'll be late if we don't leave now!" Tegan exclaimed, ducking to gather up her forgotten books. "Come on, Neval!"

Wordless, Neval bent to help her gather the books before dutifully following, still not trusting himself to speak.

"Have fun, you two," Rowan called, turning toward the blacksmith's shop.

"Oh, we will!" Tegan called, grinning widely. "We're starting *The Ballads of Leon* today!"

Rowan shuddered in mock horror before murmuring something about torture supposedly being illegal.

Tegan rolled her eyes and grabbed Neval's hand, tugging him up the hill and banishing any further possibility of conversation with her very touch.

CHAPTER

TWO

D ew clung to the hem of Neval's trousers as he walked beside Tegan along the dirt path toward the schoolhouse. Morning light filtered through the leaves, casting dappled shadows that danced over Tegan's freckled nose. Neval tried not to notice.

"How'd the reading go last night?" she asked suddenly. "I'm sorry I couldn't come over. Mam needed help in the store."

Tegan blushed slightly, which he suspected meant she'd actually been forbidden to come. Tegan's parents had never liked the idea of their darling daughter cavorting with the likes of him.

"It's fine," he muttered, keeping his eyes fixed on the path ahead.

"You finished though? Made it through ok?"

Neval let out a noncommittal grunt.

"Neval —"

"Couldn't make the words stick." He shrugged, attempting nonchalance, even as his heart raced at the thought of stumbling through the recitation. For as long as Neval could remember, reading had been a torment. Letters had always seemed to scatter across the page, and nothing he could do would make them hold still.

Without a word, Tegan halted on the path, delving into her

bag to rummage past ink-stained scrolls and a pouch of dried berries.

"What are you — "

But before he could ask, Tegan emerged with a weathered copy of *The Ballads of Leon*, its cover worn from use, and flipped it open.

> *"In the ruins of my kingdom, stand I alone,*
> *My empire fallen, my power flown.*
> *From ashes and sorrow, my spirit calls,*
> *Through shattered dreams and crumbled walls."*

Neval closed his eyes, letting the rhythm of her voice etch the words into his memory. Tegan read with clarity, each syllable a lifeline thrown across the chasm of his dread. His chest swelled with silent gratitude. How many times had they performed this same ritual? Without being asked, Tegan would read aloud to spare him the humiliation of trying to read in public. Before Rowan, before everything, she had always been there for him, and he for her — Neval and Tegan against the world.

> *"Beneath the silvered moonlight's glow,*
> *Upon dappled skin, life's light lies low.*
> *'Twixt love and death, one champion stands,*
> *Bound by unseen, ethereal bands."*

"All set?" she asked, after finishing the passage. The school-house came fully into view as they topped the last hill.

"Got it," Neval echoed, though he knew he'd need a few more repetitions to be sure. He had a sharp memory, but the torments of the classroom had a way of making words fly right out of his head.

"Good." She shot him an infectious grin that Neval couldn't help but return. Then she shook her head, brow furrowing as she pondered the lines she'd just spoken aloud. "Leon sure was batty, though."

Neval snorted. "Batty?"

"What else do you call a man who surrenders a kingdom for

love? And for some *she-wolf* who ends up dying in the end?" Tegan's voice rose in disbelief. "I mean, really?"

"Love makes you do strange things," Neval replied, his wry tone hiding the tremor of truth the words sent coursing through him. After all, if not for Tegan, he certainly wouldn't be subjecting himself to the daily humiliations of the average school day. Even if the alternative at home was arguably worse.

Tegan sighed heavily, bringing Neval back to the present. "Aren't there more important things than love?" she muttered, more to herself than to him.

Neval eyed her curiously and had just about worked up the courage to ask what she meant when she continued.

"Neval," Tegan whispered, voice wavering. "Do you ever feel trapped?"

Neval froze.

"Trapped?" His heart skipped, sensing the precarious ground ahead.

"By . . . expectations." Tegan's eyes, usually so bright, were clouded with a hint of sadness as her gaze swept over the landscape. Her fingers twitched at her side, as if longing to reach out and touch the wildness of the mountains and forests that held their small upland village. "What if there's somewhere else, somewhere . . . better?"

Neval didn't trust himself to speak, so merely nodded in encouragement.

"I'm supposed to marry Rowan," she said, twisting the hem of her cloak. "I care for him, I do. You know I do. It's just —"

Her voice trailed off, and Neval shifted on his feet, thrusting his hands deep in his pockets. "Rowan is my best friend," he offered cautiously. "And yours. He cares for you too, Tegan. Deeply."

Tegan bit her lip again. "I know that," she insisted. "Really, I do. It's just that word . . . *care*." Her face twisted, tasting the word like it was bitter on her tongue. "That's not the same as love, is it? Not really."

Neval had no words at that, even as some traitorous part deep within him silently rejoiced. Tegan had taken to pacing, running a hand through her honey curls like she did whenever she was stressed or annoyed.

"Rowan loves the uplands, Neval. He's learning a trade and he has a home here, and no desire to ever leave. Which, of course, is perfectly fine with my parents," she added ruefully. "But . . . what if I want more than that?"

Neval swallowed. "You mean like your . . . writing?" Rowan might not have qualms about referencing the Crimson Quill outright, but Neval couldn't shake the uneasy feeling that they were always being watched — no doubt from spending his entire life under occupation.

Tegan pursed her lips for a moment before sighing. "I think I started the Quill because I just needed to *do* something, Neval. For the uplands sure, but mostly just . . . for *me*."

Her eyes searched his for a long moment. "What would you do if you could choose any path?"

Neval's pulse quickened, and he swallowed thickly, shooting Tegan a glance from the corner of his eye.

"I'd . . . build," he admitted. "Design, I mean. I'd create temples and castles that touch the sky, standing long after you and I are both dust."

Neval held his breath, waiting for the laughter. After all, who'd hire an illiterate to do something so important?

"An architect," Tegan breathed, a smile breaking through. "That's perfect for you."

Something warm and buoyant filled Neval's chest, making him want to crow to the rooftops. But all he managed was a nod and a smile.

"Imagine that," Tegan mused. "A world where you create, and I . . . " Her voice trailed off, but he saw the fire ignite behind her eyes.

"Where you can be anything," he finished for her.

"Anything," she whispered, a silent agreement etching itself in the air between them. Her eyes, blazing with reckless anticipation and hope, gazed up at him and Neval couldn't help but draw closer, desperate to let her light encompass them both.

And as the moments passed, something in the air shifted. The very atmosphere around them seemed charged with this secret pact, crackling and popping with unspoken possibilities. Tegan gazed up at him through hooded lashes and a heavy warmth settled deep in Neval's stomach. He ached to touch her, to run a thumb along the softness of her cheekbone, to sink into her and never let go. But something held him back.

No, he reminded himself, *someone*.

Tegan's eyes widened almost imperceptibly, as if she too felt the possibility in this moment. She bit her bottom lip, and Neval's eyes immediately tracked the movement, the warmth in his stomach growing to a dull ache.

"Neval, I —"

The clang of the final bell from the schoolhouse shattered the moment, a stark reminder that the world did not pause for dreamers and certain harsh realities were impossible to avoid. Neval nearly groaned aloud.

"By the ancients," Tegan exclaimed. "We're actually late now!"

The spell broken, Neval turned to follow her toward the schoolhouse. But before he could move, Tegan's warm hand slipped into his, and gave his fingers a light squeeze.

"To be continued," she promised, offering a cautious smile.

Neval swallowed a lump in his throat and nodded. And as the two of them ran toward the schoolhouse, Neval felt a sense of lightness and confidence wash over him. No matter what challenges lay ahead, he knew they would face them together like they always had — Neval and Tegan against the world.

THE SCENE inside the school was a madhouse. Wherever he looked, students clambered over chairs, perching on desks and calling out to their friends. Most were boys and Tegan rolled her eyes as they passed, heading as usual for the back of the room. She was one of the few female holdouts at her age, thanks no doubt to her merchant father and her family's wealth. They certainly didn't need the extra coin her work might provide. As far as they were concerned, if their youngest child and only daughter wished to waste away her days in a stuffy schoolroom until she found herself a good husband, then that was fine by them.

At the back, they found the rest of the misfits—children of the peasant farmers that dotted the landscape around Ceffí and the few young girls whose parents saw fit to have their daughters educated. All were gazing in wide-eyed alarm at the havoc before them. Neval wordlessly followed Tegan past the faded tapestries that dotted the stone walls, sliding onto the worn wooden bench beside her.

"Well, now that you've all seen fit to join us today," the teacher drawled in a nasal voice, "we will finally begin our exploration of *The Ballads of Leon*." Neval averted his eyes from the monk's coal-black eyes, sharp and unforgiving beneath that hairless head. Brother Ludin had always given him the creeps. Devoid of eyebrows and even lashes, the monk's face had an oddly expressionless quality. Behind him, the crest of the Marian Empire loomed large, lest the upland children forget exactly who paid for (and controlled) their education.

Beside him, Tegan eagerly cracked open the brand-new copy of the ancient story. Neval's palms grew clammy at the thought of stumbling through the recitation, his mind filling with a storm of anxiety.

Subtly, Tegan nudged her book in between them.

Neval felt himself flooded anew with gratitude and affection for his friend and he shot her a grateful smile. She feigned absorption in the text, but he could just make out a tug at the corner of her mouth. He fought the sudden insane urge to run a thumb along it. He gripped the edge of his seat and forced himself to focus on the ancient text before him.

Neval tried to make sense of it. He really did. Yet as always, the letters of the ancient text seemed to swim before him and Neval turned his attention instead to the lyrical words as they were spoken aloud.

"Arnst, you will begin."

"My heart, my she-wolf, fierce and bold,

Binder of spirits, summoner of old.
Thy voice, it breaks the stones with ease,
Thy might, the terror of our enemies."

Neval's mind drifted, his fingers picking up his nub of pencil with neither thought nor command as it flew over his scrap of paper.

"Excellent. Frederick, you'll take the next stanza."

"Our love, a blaze too fierce to tame,
A river wild no banks can claim.
A tempest that in fury spins,
A sun that burns, a moon that grins."

Neval's gaze narrowed in on each stroke. He could see the magnificent building clearly in his mind—its vaulted ceilings and great flying buttresses. The angles and lines were so clear to him and he felt them spring to life on the page in front of him.

He imagined what it would be like to construct such a building, to finally see the inner workings of his mind made tangible in wood and stone. It was a dream, a fantastical dream of a life far from Ceffi's river shores, and as unattainable as the moon.

"Doodling again are we, Mr. Brennan?" A nasal voice from above him demanded. Neval jumped, jerking a hand to hide the evidence of his wandering mind—too slowly. Ludin's pale spidery hand snaked out from his blood-red robes, snatching the scrap of parchment from Neval's grip.

"So what do we have today, Mr. Brennan?" Ludin's thin lips curled in a sneer as his soulless eyes scanned the lines of Neval's rough sketch.

"It's nothing, Sir," Neval said hurriedly. "Only the story made me think—"

"Oh really? Please tell us. Share with us all what deep insights you alone gleaned from this text of the ancients, Mr. Brennan. You've clearly been hard at work."

Brother Ludin held Neval's parchment between two fingers as if it were something foul and the class erupted in laughter. Neval's ears burned, and he gritted his teeth, staring resolutely at the desk in front of him as the guffaws fell like blows.

"No? Well then, at the very least, have the courtesy of reading the next passage for the class."

Beads of sweat sprung to Neval's brow and he swallowed thickly. He turned, movements slowed by mounting dread to the text before him. He blinked rapidly, willing the letters to still, to rearrange into some semblance of order that he might make sense of.

"In—in the ru—runs,"

"*Ruins*," Tegan hissed beside him.

"In the *ruins*," Neval hastily corrected. "O—of my kin—kingdom, sand I . . . I mean *stand* I."

There was chittering from the front of the class, and the pulsating in Neval's ears shifted to a throbbing in his head as he squinted his eyes, praying the letters stopped their stumbling dance across the page.

"Stand I . . . anole?"

"*Alone*," Tegan whispered.

"That's *enough*, Miss Rourke." Ludin snarled. "If you must insist on being such an inane know-it-all, perhaps you'll do us all the courtesy of being so *elsewhere*."

Beside Neval, Tegan seemed to curl in on herself beneath the ire of the teacher's words, her eyes blinking furiously as she stared down at her lap. Neval's face warmed.

"Continue, Mr. Brennan."

Neval swallowed.

"My em—pire f—fallen, my p—plower."

"*Plower*?" A boy from the front of the class exclaimed. "Well gutter rat Brennan's got to know all about *plowers*, now wouldn't he?"

The class erupted into guffaws and Neval clamped his jaw shut, squeezing the ledge of the seat until he thought his nails might cut through.

"That's quite enough *disruption* for today, Mr. Brennan," Ludin said sharply. "Either you insist on making a mockery of this class or you are quite as stupid as you seem."

More laughter echoed around the room. Humiliation oozed through Neval, leaving a sharp tang in his mouth and a roiling in his gut. Beside him, Tegan quivered with barely controlled rage. *Don't do it*, he pleaded, silently begging her not to stand up for him. He didn't think he could take it.

Ludin turned to glide toward the front of the classroom, but not before Neval caught the smirk that pulled at his lips, the sour satisfaction that seemed to come only from the humiliation of others. Fury flared in Neval's gut and before he could stop himself, he blurted out none too quietly, "At least I'm not a hairless weasel."

Ludin's retreating back stiffened as the class once more roared with laughter. Neval didn't even think the joke was that funny but felt himself flush with pleasure at his classmates' approval. Even Tegan was trying to hide a small smile.

Neval thought he might fly.

"*What* did you say?" Icy steel coursed through Ludin's voice, bringing Neval crashing back to reality as the red-robed monk slowly rounded on him, black eyes narrowed into slits. Neval swallowed with some difficulty, but refused to look away from Ludin's burning gaze.

"Ahh, the birdie falls silent. Tell me, what is the matter?" Ludin hissed, his tall, rail-thin frame slowly advancing on Neval, a viper cornering its prey.

Neval swallowed hard and shook his head, staring resolutely at the desk before him.

"Hmm, typical. He who chirps the most has the least to contribute. And here you are playing the fool to hide the emptiness inside your own skull."

Neval gaped up at him, feeling his cheeks flame as the class fell deadly silent. But the schoolmaster was far from finished. "No, your words are nothing. *You* are nothing. Nothing but the idiot son of the town drunk. You were born in this stinking village and you will die in it, having amounted to *absolutely nothing*."

Each syllable landed like a blow and Neval's chest ached as he inhaled deeply, trying and failing to ignore the sudden roaring in his ears. His eyes shot from face to face, his panic rising in his throat as his stomach churned with shame. He was nothing. He knew it, and so did they.

Neval didn't remember jumping to his feet, nor shoving the desk away. The next thing he knew, he was outside, running like he never had before. And Neval knew he'd never be back.

CHAPTER

THREE

Neval barely heard the crash of the door behind him as he barreled out of the schoolhouse, his long legs taking the stairs in one step.

Every inch of him quivered with barely contained fury as he stood in the schoolyard. The dappled sunlight of the morning was long gone, replaced instead by a rainy mist that fell around him. No clue what to do or where to go now, Neval did the only thing left to him—he started walking. Eyes glazed, he barely processed his surroundings, the roaring in his ears blocking out everything and everyone.

He'd barely made it down the hill to the edge of the village before the soft patter of running feet behind him made him finally pause. He turned reluctantly to see Tegan, hair askew and face flushed, nearly barrel into him. She pulled up short, eyes wide as she stared at him.

"Neval—" she started, then stopped, eyes searching his with an almost frantic desperation. Then, without warning or preamble, she stepped forward and wrapped her arms around him, burying her face in his chest as if to block out the world.

He stiffened, mind going blank as they stood there, the tall pines around them doing little to block the soft drizzle of rain that coated their hair with dew.

Undeterred, Tegan's grip tightened furiously.

Ever so slowly, he wrapped his arms around her, chin resting gently on the top of her head. He let himself inhale the scent of spice and pine that was so uniquely Tegan.

Inch by inch, his muscles uncoiled, breath deepening and becoming steadier with each exhale.

He didn't know how long they stood like that, wishing more than anything that it would never end. But with each passing minute, the sights and sounds of the village encroached on their quiet world of two.

Across the road, a young boy and girl squealed over a contentious game of hacky sack. Their peals of laughter and shouts of protest echoed toward Neval and Tegan.

"That used to be us," Neval murmured, surprised by the roughness of his own voice. She turned her head, arms still gripping him, to look over at the children.

"It was," she agreed. "You were always the smartest person I knew. Still are."

Neval said nothing, but felt a flush creeping up from his neckline.

Tegan's pity was the last thing he wanted.

As if sensing his discomfort, she stepped back and grabbed his shoulders. Neval yelped in surprise as her fingers dug furiously into him.

"I'll say it 'till you believe it, Neval Brennan."

Tegan's eyes narrowed.

"You are the smartest person I've ever known and way smarter than that hook-nosed, hairless monk will ever be."

A smile tugged at Neval's lips. He'd never known Tegan to insult anyone, and especially not a teacher.

Grinning triumphantly, Tegan barreled on. "So what if reading isn't your strong suit? You're an incredible artist, Neval! And you finish your maths faster than any of us. Your one struggle does not define your worth. It merely enables your triumph."

Against his better judgment, Neval let her words settle over him, pulling them tight to keep out the battering winds.

Tegan had always had a way of calming him, helping him shut out the world with all its cruelties and injustices. Even on the darkest day of his life, she'd been there to hold him as he wept into her lap. He still remembered it—the day his mother died. Curling up in the cave behind the creek inlet that was all their own. Remembered the hard stone of the ground and the feel of her tears falling on his head, mixing with his own as they each wept their sorrow into the wordless echoes of the damp cave walls.

The children's shouts startled Neval from his reverie, as a wayward kick sent their ball flying toward him and Tegan. Instinctively, he dropped her embrace to catch it, but missed her warmth as soon as it was gone. Hiding his regret, he stepped forward, offering the boy a warm smile as he ran up to retrieve it. The boy smiled hesitantly in return.

"Looks like you had a decent streak going," Neval said, nodding toward the girl, now happily tracing designs into the dirt with a stick.

The boy's grin widened and he puffed out his chest slightly, saying. "I'm the hacky sack king, you know. I can keep it going for over a hundred!"

Neval whistled appreciatively.

"Salina's still learnin' though, and she needs a little more . . . practice."

He said this last as a whisper and Tegan muffled a snort.

Neval elbowed her in the ribs and nodded, all seriousness to match the boy's own.

"You'll have to keep practicing then. Don't neglect your friends, though. They're the best thing you've got."

Beside him, Tegan had stopped laughing and now leaned gently into him.

"Sure thing!" the boy said brightly. "We always go to—"

"Edgar James, *what* are you doing?"

The undeniably maternal screech came from across the road and Neval glanced up to see a portly woman standing next to an abashed Salina, hands perched firmly on her hips. Shooting Neval an apologetic grimace, Ewan turned on his heels and sprinted back to his mother, only to be met with a firm box around the ears.

"What you doin' hangin' round that trash?" his mother

demanded. "No good'll come from the likes of him. Mark my words."

Edgar nodded obediently, him and Salina following her without a backwards glance. A warm flush spread across Neval's cheeks as a familiar roaring filled his ears. He tried desperately to recapture his calm, the breath that had come so easily now burning his nostrils. He couldn't be here anymore, not now, not ever.

"It's not you," Tegan whispered, almost pleaded. Her eyes were round and her fingers grazed his tunic as he pushed past. "It's just your f—"

"I know exactly what it is—" he snapped. "—why they hate me. I don't need you, of all people, explaining it to me."

Tegan blinked, mouth parting slightly.

"I only meant—" Tegan paused, shaking her head. "Let's get out of here, Neval. We can go to the river, just like in the old days. Wouldn't that be nice?"

Her words were a salve meant to cool the smarting flesh of his injured pride. And though he begrudged them purchase, he could feel them working. For a moment, Neval let himself return to those memories—long summer days sprinting through the forest, only to crash into cool river water, their childish shrieks as the icy water met their flesh. In those days it was just him and Tegan, free to play without care for their differences in station or the strains of adolescence, before Rowan's family moved to the village, before . . . everything.

Neval's chest ached with longing. What would he give to return to those days? Days when their most pressing concern was whether Mrs. Flaugherty would sneak them some spare mutton pie at day's end.

"I miss those days," Tegan whispered, catching his line of thought. A shy smile tugged at her lips as she squeezed his arm gently. "Don't you?"

The image shifted in Neval's mind and he let it, feeling his muscles relax ever so slightly.

It would be just like old times.

He imagined racing Tegan to the river today, her peals of

laughter echoing through the branches as she dodged the mud cakes he always threw at her. He imagined them stripping down and sinking into cool waves, the scratchy wool of their clothes abandoned on the shore bed. He could see the curve of Tegan's hips as she sunk beneath —

A sudden ache in his stomach made every muscle in Neval's body stiffen.

Oh, Pneumos curse it —

He yanked his arm away, ignoring Tegan's wide blinking eyes, confusion swirling in their depths.

His hand shot guiltily to the knife at his belt, gripping it until the notches cut into his palm, notches he and Rowan had carved together—one for each bully he'd helped Neval face. Rowan may not have been Neval's oldest friend, but he was loyal and kind and he deserved better than this. Neval couldn't think this way about Tegan.

Those long summer days of childhood were gone, never to return since the first time Tegan and Rowan truly locked eyes on each other. When their twosome had become a threesome. Neval had been so grateful for another friend, he'd never stopped to think what it might cost him. When Rowan and Tegan began courting, he told himself he didn't care, that he was happy for them. And on some level, he was. But that was a long time ago, and the years had a way of adding weight with their passing and the old wound never truly healed.

Tegan was still staring at him, surprise and confusion etched on her face.

"Neval—"

"I don't expect you to understand, Tegan." Neval said coldly. "We can't all be beloved."

When she opened her mouth to reply, he pushed past her. "Besides, I have to go. Some of us have actual chores to do, Tegan. We can't all be free to just shoot the breeze on daddy's money."

From the corner of his eye, he saw Tegan blush scarlet, her lips parting as she stared at him like he'd slapped her. And maybe, just maybe, he saw the soft glaze of tears in her eyes. He didn't stop to check.

He couldn't be here anymore, not when his blood pulsed in his ears, throbbing in his stomach like it might explode out of him. The villagers of Ceffí hated him—always had, always would. And sooner or later, Tegan would look at him with that same loathing. He wasn't about to wait around until then.

If all these folks thought him nothing more than trouble-making trash, he'd be happy to oblige. There was no place for him here, not for someone like him. So he trudged onward, leaving Tegan far behind.

EXHAUSTION WEIGHED HEAVILY on him as he trudged across the thick mud of the barren field, each step an effort as he sunk further into the clinging mud. Ahead the crumbling shack stood desolate, devoid of light or life. Neval paused, a mixture of dread and anxiety swirling in his chest as he stared at the hovel. He spent most of his time avoiding his so-called home, preferring instead to pass the hours with either Tegan or Rowan. But that wasn't exactly an option now.

A low rumble echoed through the air and Neval glanced up just in time for thick drops of water to land on his face. He let them roll across his skin for a moment, breathing in the tangy electricity that made the hair on the back of his neck stand on end. But as the rain came harder, he realized there was no use delaying the inevitable. He trudged toward the shack.

Inside, the harsh acidic smell of brewed mogda assaulted his senses, threatening to burn his nares as he inhaled. The faint scent of pandry smoke was already beginning to fade—the last of the expensive vice burned away weeks ago, along with the rest of their savings. Now all that remained was that home-brewed acid.

The shack held scant furniture—an overturned table and benches, a copper cooking pot over an extinguished fire, and a half-collapsed bed with a loudly snoring lump buried in its depths. Neval's eyes flicked instinctively to the only thing of beauty in the dirt-covered hovel—a beautifully painted vase perched on the mantel where a warm fire used to crackle and pop.

Delicate lilies swirled across its surface and Neval couldn't help the memories that came with it—his child-like hand clutching the brush, his mother's graceful fingers guiding his over the vase's smooth surface, her warm words of praise at his success, kind words of encouragement in his struggle —

Neval blinked away the memories, swallowing hard against the lump that rose in his throat.

She's gone, he reminded himself. *And it's your fault.*

Neval let the door slam shut with a crash and smirked in satisfaction as the man in the bed sat bolt upright. Satisfaction quickly turned to dismay as the shadowed figure blindly swung at some unseen adversary and rolled gracelessly out of bed, landing with a thump and a resounding roar in a pile off the side.

Neval stared at Erik Brennan in disgust as he crawled out from beneath tattered bed linens and staggered to his feet, resenting the mousy brown hair and crooked nose they shared. Slowly, his father made his way toward the barrel next to the now banked fire, cursing as he tripped over the upturned bench. His bloodshot eyes turned to Neval, straining to focus.

"What're you doin' 'ere boy? Don't you 'ave chores or somethin'?" Even his words were sluggish, his tongue tripping over every syllable.

"I had school," Neval replied shortly, not bothering to explain why he was back in the middle of the day. Erik certainly didn't know the time.

"Hmm," his father grunted, rubbing a filthy rag across his face. Neval's nose curled in disgust. This was his heritage, he realized, a life of worthless struggle only to die at the bottom of a mogda barrel. The brew was an Uplander specialty, the potent combination of fermented river cane both cheap to buy and dangerously easy to make. And there was nothing like it for drowning their sorrows, hiding their collective tears, and forgetting their shame. It was, he knew, truly the drink of his people. And his father was an expert.

The sharp sting of disappointment flickered in his chest as he looked at his father—an embarrassment to the village and no doubt half the reason Neval himself was so hated. Forever guilty by association as the son of the town drunk.

Whether it was the ordeal in the schoolhouse or just a foul mood after his argument with Tegan, something finally broke within him.

"What about you then? I can see from the field it isn't ready for sowing. Not even plowed—"

His father blinked at him, a brief clarity suddenly filling those eyes. Neval swallowed nervously.

"What did you say t'me?" his father demanded slowly, carefully annunciating each word as if he couldn't quite believe what he'd heard. He wasn't alone.

"I only meant—"

"Oh, I know what you meant, you ungrateful child. We lost everythin' after the last rising, when those damn red cloaks burned everythin' out of spite. And what 'ave I done since then if not provided for you, put a roof over your head, food on the table —"

"Don't forget the endless tankards of mogda," Neval muttered under his breath.

"What was that?" his father asked. Neval wasn't sure what came over him, but he spat back, "I said don't forget your preferred drink, Da. And good thing Ma isn't here to see exactly what you've become."

As soon as the words left his mouth, Neval regretted them. He stared in budding horror as Erik's face turned twelve shades of purple. He'd really done it now.

"That's it! Get out! Get out of here, boy!" his father roared. With surprising dexterity, he grabbed for the vase on the mantel, fingers curling around its slender neck.

"No, don't!" Neval cried, but it was too late.

Neval ducked just in time as the vase sailed into the wall behind him, the shower of shattered ceramic falling in rivulets down his back as he lay sprawled on the floor.

He curled up there for a moment, paralyzed in the same position he always seemed to find himself in, the hard-packed dirt of the shack's floor a familiar discomfort and the shuffle and slamming of a mug on the table a well-known refrain.

Not anymore.

He was done with this life. Finished with the floor and the fear that came with it. He was tired of the mockery, done with the disdain. There was a better life out there for him. His mother had promised him as much.

Slowly, he uncurled and climbed into a kneeling position on the floor, scooping up a large piece of the shattered ceramic, the one thing of his mother's he had left. Neval traced the flower with a thumb, the delicate lilac petals he'd helped his mother paint, and swallowed the salty tears that sprung to his eyes. Brushing furiously at his face lest his father see, Neval's hand curled around the ceramic shard so that its sharp edges cut deep into his palm. Unwilling to look back, he stood and strode to the door, wrenching it open as the wind howled and rain pelted into the tiny shack. Behind him, his father cursed but Neval ignored him, striding out into the deluge.

He found the plow easily enough, lying unused as it always did against the shack's wall, exposed for all the elements and any bold thief. He couldn't say what drove him, some last remnant of his mother's voice begging him not to leave his father with nothing. So, gripping the roughhewn wood, Neval dragged the plow to the field. Ignoring the icy sting of the pelting rain, he moved his hands into place along the old handles, worn smooth from years of work. He slipped the harness over his head, binding himself to the machine, to the only path he'd ever been good for. He slid the plow's blade into the mud, and heaving with all his strength, cut a path through its muddy depths. The rain pelted mercilessly, but still Neval pushed on. Aided by neither horse nor ox, he carried on for the hours that followed.

When he'd reached the end of the last row, he let the plow tumble to the side as he collapsed onto the grass. Already soaked through, he lay still, panting and shivering against the pelting rain and howling wind.

He'd done it, he realized. The field was plowed and ready for sowing. But this was as far as he went—the last thing he ever did for his miserable excuse for a father. It was time to leave, he told himself. How long had he thought about it? Fantasized about taking to the road in search of a better life, any life but this one. And now it was time. He'd find a town somewhere, an architect or even just a builder he could apprentice himself to. It would be hard, and many would doubt him. He'd face cold nights and hungry days, but what else was new?

But he'd be a person, not just the outward sign of his father's failures, the town's idiot troublemaker expected to amount to nothing more than the town drunk—a disgrace. No, he'd be someone else, someone worthy of respect.

And as Neval lay in the mud, pelted by rain and frozen to the bone, he laughed, because the future could hold nothing worse than where he'd come from.

CHAPTER

FOUR

The sun came early and insistent the following morning and Neval blinked groggily against the rays that filtered through the cracked and filthy windows of the shack. He rolled over, easing onto his feet from where he'd slept, curled up before the fireplace. He shouldn't have worried. If the snoring mound from the bed was any sign, his father wouldn't be up for several more hours.

Neval stood there for a moment, weighing his resolve from the night before. After all, how many times before had he sworn he was through—finished with this life and done living under his father's oppressive control, only to wake up the following morning filled with the same doubts and fears?

But this time was different. The fear was still there. After all, what was he supposed to do in the wider world of Loren, where no one knew him from the next out-of-work peasant? Who would trust him enough to give him a job? Though the villagers in Ceffí may hate him for his father's reputation and the various debts he left festering in his wake, at least Neval wasn't a stranger and had some way of making a living, scrawny though it might be.

But no. With every passing day, Neval felt his soul die a little more. And what little hope that remained slipped away with every passing insult and indignity.

So Neval set about scouring the shack for anything that might

29

be of use. Barren though it was, he still managed to ferret away a small hatchet and a few moldy blocks of cheese. Silently slipping from the shack, Neval set out down the path toward the school-house, his sack thumping with a satisfying thwack against his shoulder blades with each step.

This is it, he thought. *I'm finally on my way.*

His stomach fluttered with giddy nerves at the thought, satisfaction blooming with every step he took away from the shack that had been like a prison ever since his mother's death.

His feet slowed to a stop as he approached the path's intersection with the road. To the south lay the sea and the city of Karthaíla, likely his best chance at making a fresh start, terrifying as the thought of a large city might be.

Yet almost without thought, Neval glanced north toward Ceffí. It was almost time for school to start, and he knew Rowan and Tegan would be waiting for him at the fork just outside town where the road branched up the hill toward the school, just as they were every day.

My friends, Neval thought, pain and regret making his chest tight.

I have to at least say goodbye.

So, his steps heavy with defeat, Neval turned back toward Ceffí, trying to ignore the flutter of panic that filled his chest as he returned to the place that had filled his life with such pain. But he had to say goodbye. He owed them that at least, the two best things in his life for so many years.

Lost in his own reverie, Neval nearly missed the rhythmic pounding of hoofbeats that descended from behind him.

"CLEAR THE ROAD!" A voice bellowed, and Neval barely had time to stumble into the ditch off the side before an entire cadre of red-cloaked Bellators galloped past, heading north toward Ceffí.

Dusting himself off, Neval stared after them, wondering what in the world might send so many Bellators this far from the cities. He'd long since accepted the military's presence in Ceffí, a daily reminder that their lives weren't really their own. But their numbers had always been small, no doubt having better things to occupy their time than police a small upland village.

Something churned in Neval's stomach, though he couldn't say just what. Yet he picked up his pace to a jog as he hurried on toward the village. Something was happening and he was determined to find out what.

A crowd had already gathered in the village center when Neval arrived and caught sight of Rowan and Tegan waving him over.

"What's happened?" he asked, pushing toward them and only slightly out of breath.

"No idea," Rowan muttered, scowling as he crossed his arms over his wide chest, "but it can't be nothin' good."

At his side, Tegan stood twisting a lock of hair between her fingers as her eyes darted between the assembled Bellators. At their center, a tall, graying Bellator nailed a piece of parchment to the side of the well post, each thwack sending the rickety structure quivering in protest. He turned then and his piercing gray eyes scanned the assembled crowd warily.

"My name is Millus Flavius," he began, his gruff voice carrying across the village square, though he hardly raised his voice. The low rumble of the villagers quieted immediately in response.

"The Empire has charged me with overseeing security for the construction of the Karthaíla Dam. In this vein—"

The collective gasp of the crowd cut off his words, and was immediately followed by a cacophony of protests, questions, and accusations from the villagers of Ceffí.

"What!"

"You can't possibly expect—"

"Why now?"

"It won't stand!" Rowan bellowed, turning red in the face. Tegan and Neval simultaneously laid a steadying hand on each arm.

"How d'you expect us to make a living?" This came from Farmer Anderson, clutching the reins and making his donkey balk at the tight hold.

"What about our l'il ones?" Laoise, the baker's wife, demanded. She clutched two small dirt-covered children to her side even as she bounced a squawking baby on her hip.

The protests continued for several minutes as the Millus, now looking very much annoyed, tried in vain to regain control of the situation.

"ENOUGH!" He finally bellowed, gesturing for his Bellators to step forward, swords partially unsheathed in an unmistakably menacing manner.

The villagers' protests finally settled into an uneasy murmur as they all waited uneasily for the Millus to continue.

"The plans *will* move forward as scheduled. This project has been decided by those far higher up than I, and though you all may have your concerns, ultimately you must accept that it is *indeed* happening." With these words, Millus Flavius eyed each person sternly, daring them to contradict him. "As I said, I've been placed in charge of security, and I have no patience for malcontents or troublemakers. I've ordered an entire centurium to be stationed here in Ceffí under the command of Centus Gregori."

At his words, a much shorter man stepped forward. Stockily built with a pinched face forever frozen into a scowl, Gregori eyed the villagers with nothing short of disdain.

"He will be fair," Flavius continued, shooting a wary glance at his scowling lieutenant. "But you *will* heed his orders. *Nothing* and *no-one* will impede the progress of construction." Though he said the words calmly, the threat was clear.

Neval shot a wary glance at Rowan, still fuming beside him, silently imploring him to keep his fool mouth shut. Now was definitely *not* the time to paint a giant target on his back.

Though the crowd still hummed with muttered resentment, no one resumed their shouting. Clearly satisfied, Millus Flavius ordered that they disperse immediately. The crowd complied, their whispered conversations buzzing throughout the village square as they all returned to their business of the day.

Neval turned with Tegan and Rowan and the three of them made their way toward the schoolhouse.

"Why start the Karthaíla Dam now?" Tegan asked quietly after a moment. "After . . . *everything*."

"*Everything* being a massive *screw you* from our Marian overlords?" Rowan spat, venomously eyeing the groups of two and three Bellators taking up their positions around the square.

"There has to be a reason, though." Tegan began. "They have to expect there'll be resistance."

"And when has that ever stopped them?" Rowan muttered darkly.

Neval and Tegan exchanged a glance, both thinking the same thing. Rowan's father had gotten mixed up in the protests years before, shortly after his family had moved to Ceffí.

"It won't be like last time," Neval said quietly, laying a hand on Rowan's arm.

Rowan snorted, shaking him off roughly.

"Sure it will. They'll tell us again how it will improve *farmin' outputs*." Rowan didn't bother to lower his voice as they passed another group of Bellators. "They'll dam up the river to *prevent flooding* and *better control irrigation*." Rowan's voice had taken on a mocking tone at this point and Neval subtly steered them out toward the edge of the village. "Only just like last time, they'll conveniently forget to mention that the dam will go *south* of us. *We'll* be the ones flooded out," Rowan spat. "They'll make Ceffí so uninhabitable that we all just pick up and move to the cities. That's where they want us, anyway, better controlled that way." His voice had steadily risen and Neval shot him a warning glance as more Bellators passed. Rowan ignored him, boldly glaring at the red cloaked figures who thankfully didn't seem to notice—laughing instead at some discussion of a sports game back in Crîd Eálas.

"I heard there was some sort of holdup in funding for construction, so everyone hoped the idea would just go away," Neval said.

"Seems our luck's run out," Rowan muttered.

Neval and Tegan shared a glance. The three of them had arrived at their designated spot to part ways, but neither of them seemed willing to let Rowan take off in such a state.

"Rowan," Tegan whispered, "There's always—"

"And what will you do about it?" he snapped. "Write about it in your silly broadsides? What good has that done so far? Nothing ever *changes*! And it never will unless someone actually *does* something about it."

And with that, Rowan turned on his heel and stomped off toward the blacksmith's shop, shooting a sharp glare at anyone who dared get in his way. Tegan stared after him, eyes wide and blinking quickly against the glistening of tears. Neval swallowed the bitter taste of fury that coated his tongue, reminding himself that Rowan hadn't meant it.

"What did I—" Tegan asked, turning wide eyes to Neval in question. He only shook his head.

"Ignore him. Let him bang out his troubles at the forge," Neval said quietly, watching the hulking form of his friend stride down the side alley. He kicked up rocks in his path as he went, the only outlet available for his fury. "He'll be fine."

"I can't imagine what he's feeling," Tegan said quietly. "He never likes to talk about his father."

Neval nodded grimly. It had been years ago, when the three of them had been only children. Those first protestors had set up their barricade on the river, claiming they wouldn't let merchants pass until they were granted an audience with the Regio to plead their case. Well, the Bellatorio had had little patience for that — blasting apart their barricade in one go and killing several men who refused to abandon the effort. Rowan's father had been one of them.

Rowan had changed after that. No longer interested in playing with the other boys at school, he'd kept to himself, sitting alone and staring off into the distance. Neval had felt sorry for him, knowing better than most what it felt like to lose a parent. All it had taken was a shared loaf of bread over lunch and just like that, he and Tegan's duo became a trio.

"He'll need us now more than ever, Neval." Tegan said, startling him out of his memories. "You're such a good friend to him — to both of us. I don't know what we'd do without you."

Guilt churned in his gut as he watched Tegan turn and head toward the steps to the schoolhouse, its tall facade staring down at him, casting its mocking shadow. The one place he swore he'd never return to.

Sensing his hesitation, Tegan glanced back at him.

"You coming?"

"I—I'm sorry about yesterday, Tegan. I never meant—"

His voice trailed off even as Tegan's voice softened, and she reached back to grasp his hand.

"Forget about it. It was a rotten day all around. But today will be better," she said, voice determined. "We will make it so. And tonight, we'll find Rowan and give him a proper cheering up."

And with that, Neval allowed himself to be tugged inside the schoolhouse.

Tonight, he thought. *I'll tell them both tonight. I'll tell them I'm leaving for good.*

CHAPTER

FIVE

The school day passed with surprisingly little humiliation, although with minimal productivity. Even Ludin seemed distracted by the morning's events, fiddling with the chain around his neck and glancing compulsively out the window with every passing noise. He finally gave up, sending them off to study the day's lesson on their own while he began scratching out letters on his desk.

No doubt seeking new employment in some other unsuspecting village, Neval thought bitterly. The rest of the day passed in nervous anticipation, and the class spilled from the schoolhouse as soon as the designated hour arrived. They waited in their usual spot at the crossroads just outside town for Rowan to finish up work and join them. But the hours of the day ticked on with no sign of their friend.

Hopefully, the fool didn't get himself in trouble, Neval thought.

He glanced at Tegan's tapping foot, her eyes searching the distance, and knew she was thinking the same.

"He's coming," she said firmly in answer to his sidelong glance. "Probably just got held late at the blacksmith's. A day like today, everyone must be horribly behind."

Neval nodded, though the churning in the pit of his stomach suggested otherwise. Afternoon soon turned to dusk with no sign of Rowan and Neval felt himself grow antsy. It was now or never.

He had to leave now if he wanted to make it to shelter before nightfall.

Swallowing, he stood up from the bench.

"I have to go, Tegan," Neval whispered.

"Just wait a bit longer," Tegan said, still searching the rapidly darkening street. "We'll walk you back to the farm after."

Neval swallowed. It had to be now.

"I'm not going back to the farm, Tegan. I—I'm leaving, for good this time."

This finally caught her attention.

"Wh-what are you talking about? You can't just leave, Neval. Ceffí is your home."

Neval's jaw clenched and he forced himself to remain calm.

"It's not, Tegan. You know that. Not since—" he paused, fighting the swirl of emotions that always seemed to well up at the most inconvenient times. "Well, not for a long while now. It's time I leave and I'm going—*tonight*."

He said this last with what he hoped was steady confidence, but her disbelieving expression only settled into a scowl.

"What did that bastard do?"

Neval gaped at her. He could count on one hand how many times he'd heard Tegan curse.

"Wh-what? Nothing — "

"Don't lie to me, Neval. What did your father do to you?"

His jaw clenched as he met her searching expression and he shook his head jerkily. "It doesn't matter."

Tegan pursed her lips as she considered him.

"You'll stay with me, then." Waving off his stuttering protest, she continued, "Father won't like it, but he can deal with it. If nothing else, the backroom of the store can be made into—"

"Tegan!" This caught her up short and he gripped her shoulders on either side. "I can't stay with you and I can't stay here. This place has nothin' for me. Surely you can see that."

Her lips thinned even further, and she glared at him, refusing to concede what they both knew to be true.

"If I stay here, I'll always be the no-good troublemaking son of the town drunk, good for nothin' but plowin' fields until I drop dead of exhaustion or hang from the noose."

He could see his words take hold, but still she shook her head.

"You're smart, Neval, the smartest person I've ever met." Her eyes glistened as she stared up at him, pleading. "Please don't go."

Neval swallowed, feeling his resolve teeter on the edge, those eyes threatening to do him in completely.

"If you believed that, Tegan," he whispered, "you'd want me to go. In a city I could start over, make something of myself in a place where no one knew what type of people I came from."

I could be an architect, he thought. *Or at the very least, a builder.*

He fought the swell of hope that unfurled in his chest at the thought. When he let himself dream like this, the world seemed to hold such possibility. He could be *anyone*, do *anything*.

His excitement threatened to carry him away, but then he caught sight of Tegan's face. For the first time, she seemed almost small, her expression pained and her eyes welling with tears. Neval realized then what Tegan had known all along, that there could be no fresh start for her. Ceffí was her life, a path laid out and waiting for her.

On a whim, Neval opened his mouth to beg her to come with him. They could start this new life together—free from Ceffí and its small-minded ways. Then an image of Rowan's devastated face floated into his mind and he stopped.

They were engaged.

Neval couldn't run away with his best friend's betrothed. He couldn't do that to one of his best friends in the world. He closed his mouth.

"Where will you go?" Tegan asked in a tiny voice. "It's almost dark already."

"The caves by the river," he said, smiling sadly. "I'll camp out there for the night, just like when we were kids."

Swallowing, Tegan nodded slowly before throwing her arms around his neck and squeezing tightly. Neval returned the embrace, trying to etch the feel of her into his mind as he struggled to swallow the lump that suddenly filled his throat. He stepped back.

"Can I — can I walk you home before I go? It's getting dark."

Tegan shook her head. "I'll stop by the tavern, I think. Rowan might have gone there after work."

It was the shot of pain that coursed through his chest at her words that finally gave him the strength to turn away. Slowly, he forced one foot in front of the other, ignoring the thudding in his chest and the roaring in his ears.

I'm really doing this.

How many nights had he lain awake dreaming of this very moment? How long had he stayed awake, ignoring the pain of his empty stomach as he listened to his father's gurgling snores? But he was finally doing it. He was leaving Ceffí.

Yet even in his jubilation, something gnawed at his stomach, a wariness he couldn't explain, but that drew his feet to a halt.

Come on, he thought. *It's now or never. I have to do this. I have to leave.* But it was Tegan's face that floated into his mind, cheeks flushed, and eyes filled with tears. He swore aloud.

She isn't mine.

How long had he hovered on the sidelines of their relationship? Watching them grow closer and closer before finally announcing their betrothal. He couldn't do it anymore, couldn't keep waiting around to watch her and Rowan get married, have a family, even. He couldn't keep feigning happiness while his heart was breaking into a million pieces.

Yet still her face floated before his vision — wonderful, kind, fierce Tegan, and he knew he couldn't leave either, not without telling her how he felt.

He was already turning around when he heard the cry of surprise and fear.

And then he was running.

CHAPTER
SIX

Neval's feet pounded the pavement as he rounded the corner, slipping over the wet stone of the main road until he crashed down onto one knee. He winced, barely registering the shooting pain up his leg as he staggered to his feet just in time to see a Bellator shove Tegan roughly against the wall of the tavern.

She cried out as the Bellator's companion laughed, sneering face illuminated by the warm light of the tavern window. Panicked, Neval slowed his pace, inching along the shadowed wall of the tannery across the road, racking his brain for some way to get them out of this.

The Bellator pressed Tegan hard against the stone wall, face inches from hers as she tried in vain to wrest herself from his grip. He murmured something in her ear, and she spat into his face. He whipped his head back, just enough so Neval could see Tegan's fierce, determined expression. Then the Bellator's fist connected hard against the side of her face, snapping her head back into the stone wall with a nauseating thud.

Panic coursed through Neval as Tegan slumped slightly against the wall, head hanging limp as she spat blood. A roaring filled his ears, muffling the sound of the Bellators' laughter. Without thinking, without planning, Neval lunged.

He tackled the first Bellator around the waist, both sprawling into the mud. The Bellator smelled of sweat and brewed mogda and Neval rolled to avoid a wild and too-slow punch from the inebriated man.

Only half thinking, Neval's fist flew, landing solidly in soft flesh. The Bellator tried to shield himself, but he was still sprawled on his back and the mogda slowed his reactions. But just as Neval moved to punch the filth straight in his mouth, the Bellator seemed somehow to remember the knife at his hip.

In a blustering rage, he lunged for Neval, blade unsheathed.

Neval just managed to grab the man's meaty wrist before the force of the movement carried him backwards. Then the weight of the Bellator was on top of him and Neval felt the air squeeze from his lungs in a single rush. Writhing in all directions, Neval tried desperately to escape the man's cumbersome weight, but to no avail. All he could do was hold on for dear life, fighting the wrist that pressed the blade ever closer to his neck.

Neval's muscles screamed with effort, his joints threatening to pop under the strain. The Bellator's now-purple face pressed closer to his as he whispered, "Big mistake, uplander filth. Once you've been gutted, who'll protect her then?"

Fury coursed through him and Neval suddenly remembered his own knife, its notched handle pressed firmly into the mud beneath him. Snaking his hand free, his fingers grasped it.

In one swift movement, he had it unsheathed. Not giving himself time to think, he plunged it into the Bellator's belly— once, twice, until the man's cries twisted into gurgling sputters.

Heaving the man's weight off of him, Neval found none other than Tegan standing over him, brandishing the Bellator's own dropped blade at his gaping companion.

"Leave," she hissed through gritted teeth.

Neval scrambled to his feet to join her, both brandishing weapons toward the Bellator's no-longer leering companion. The companion's face went slack with drunken surprise and he staggered back, eyes dancing between the two of them and his friend lying dead in a puddle of his own blood. Then he turned and ran.

They stood like that for a moment, the sound of laughter and clinking glasses spilling into the street with the light of the tavern window. No one had heard a thing.

Beside him, Tegan swayed dangerously, and the knife in her hand clattered to the ground. Neval caught her just as her knees buckled.

"Come on, T," he murmured, eyes darting toward both ends of the street. "We have to get out of here — now!"

They staggered down the alleyway, putting as much distance as they could between them and the dead man. With every step, Tegan seemed to find her feet and soon they were half-walking, half-running toward the edge of town. It was only when they'd stumbled, legs aching and chests heaving into the shelter of the forest, that they collapsed in a heap under a massive oak tree.

The sound of their gasps for air filled the silence as an all-too bright moon illuminated the night air. Neval glanced over to find Tegan's shoulders shaking, just as a sob tore from her chest. He immediately went to her, wrapping an arm around her shoulders and pressing her to him. She turned toward him and buried her face in his shoulder. They stayed that way for a while, Tegan sobbing and Neval's thoughts warring between fury and heartbreak for his best friend.

Gradually, her sobs slowed and he glanced down to find Tegan staring up at him, her face mere inches from his.

He stopped breathing.

One slow tear rolled down her cheek and, without thinking, he wiped it away with his thumb, hesitating when he reached the corner of her mouth. Heat roiled in his gut, and he moved to pull away. But with one swift motion, she caught his hand, pressing it firmly to her flushed cheek.

Neval swallowed, eyes meeting hers in confusion. She gazed steadily back at him. He opened his mouth, intending something witty or disparaging, anything to break the suddenly weighted tension between them.

But whatever it was flew from his mind as Tegan leaned forward and pressed her lips to his.

Neval's body went rigid, ecstatic delight and confusion

warring within him. Her lips danced over his, light at first and then firmer, fiercer. His arms tightened instinctually around her and all Neval could think about was how warm her lips were, the salt of her tears pricking his tongue.

What are you doing? A voice asked in the back of his head. *This is Tegan. She's your friend. And Rowan, what about Rowan?*

Guilt churned in his gut, and he forced himself to pull away. Tegan's brow furrowed in confusion as she stared up at him and he braced his arms against her shoulders as much to keep himself at bay as her.

"What are we—? Tegan, I know that was awful. But are you sure you—?"

She silenced him with a finger to his lips, eyes boring into his as she whispered, "You came back."

And Neval had no words to reply, because of course he came back. It was *her.*

Her eyes seemed to register the words he couldn't quite say as she slowly wrapped her arms around his neck and pressed her lips to his. His body responded on instinct as the fire in his gut suddenly coursed through his limbs. He snaked an arm around her waist, pressing her to him and he vaguely wondered if such heat might burn her. At that moment, he didn't much care.

His other hand laced itself in her hair, and he reveled in the rich scent of her. They kissed fiercely, lips leaving fiery trails along cheeks and necks—neither stopping to think about the danger they'd both been in. In that moment, there was only the two of them and it was perfect.

Gradually their kisses became less intense, less desperate, and Tegan settled her head against his shoulder. They sat like that for a while, Neval feeling all at once happier and more relaxed than he had in years.

"They can't find you," Tegan whispered. "If they do, you're as good as dead."

Neval's heart picked up pace once more, a hammering that roared in his ears and throbbed in his head.

What have I done?

"I-I'll run. I was plannin' to leave, anyway."

Tegan's head jerked up. Though she still leaned against him, her body had stiffened, losing the relaxed posture of just moments before.

"You can't outrun the Bellatorio, Neval. They're in all the major cities. Once they realize who's missing, and they will, you know, they'll sound the alarm and nowhere will be safe."

A wave of nausea roiled in his gut and Neval put out a hand—bracing himself against the ground as a wave of lightheadedness washed over him.

This is it then, he thought. So much for a new life—dashed before it even started.

"The caves," Tegan breathed. "Go to the caves. It's hidden and they won't know to look for you there. I'll bring you food and eventually it'll all die down." Her words bore a confidence Neval wasn't sure he shared. But another fear gnawed at him, far stronger.

"What about you?" he asked. "He saw your face, too. You'll be first on their list to interrogate."

Tegan's face hardened and she replied cooly. "He won't. Not unless he wants to be accused of assault, that is."

Icy fury roared in his head, but he quickly reined it in. Now was not the time. Besides, Neval wasn't at all sure the Bellator would share such scruples and he didn't hide his doubt from his face.

"I don't want to leave you," he murmured, reaching on instinct for her hand.

Tegan's face softened and she squeezed his hands in return. "I'll be fine, Neval. Now please, go. Before anyone thinks to look for us."

Neval swallowed compulsively, searching her eyes for some clue where this left them, where the two of them went from here. But her gaze was shuttered, fixed intently on the town and this puzzle she had to solve.

Finally, he nodded and stood to go. But at the last moment,

Tegan caught his hand. He met her eyes and found them soft, warm. She squeezed his hand, and he knew then, beyond all reason, that they would be ok. They would figure this out and all would be as it should be.

With that conviction in his belly, he made for the caves.

CHAPTER

SEVEN

Well, it was official. Neval was quite possibly the worst friend ever. As he lay against the hard stone floor of the cave, staring up at the damp ceiling above, he couldn't quite bring himself to shift into a more comfortable position.

Good, he thought sourly. *You don't deserve comfort.*

He'd kissed her.

He'd actually *kissed* Tegan. How could he have done that? She was his friend, his oldest friend. And worse, she was engaged to Rowan.

The thought of Rowan sent a wave of nausea roiling through him. What was he going to do? Leave? That had been his plan from the beginning, but now the thought of sneaking off in the night made him feel even more guilty, a coward unwilling to face what he'd done. And Tegan, what would Tegan think? Maybe she regretted it? She'd been attacked, after all. Neither of them had been thinking clearly.

Neval groaned aloud.

How had things gone so terribly wrong?

The sound of crunching footsteps interrupted his mental flogging and he froze, barely daring to breathe. Neval closed his eyes, willing the steps to keep moving and the sticky darkness of the cave to swallow him whole. The footsteps stopped just outside the entrance and he cursed silently, mentally preparing to fight his way out.

"Neval?" Though uttered in a whisper, the words were loud enough to echo through the cave. Only one person could be that loud while trying to be quiet.

"I know you're here, Neval," Rowan called. "Don't worry, I'm alone."

Neval sighed, cursing whatever gods had turned their back on him. But there really was nothing for it. Rolling onto his belly, he crawled out of the cave. Emerging through dense underbrush, he saw Rowan's broad shouldered form startle and turn to see him. Neval scrambled to his feet, mouth already open to plead his case, to apologize, to self-flagellate, whatever Rowan wanted. But before he could say anything, he was engulfed in a bone-crushing hug.

"W-what?" Neval gasped.

Releasing him, Rowan held him by the shoulders at arm's length. He opened his mouth to say something, then quickly snapped it shut as his eyes caught sight of the cave opening behind him, only a few feet tall at its highest.

"Pneumos bless it. When she said a cave, I imagined something a bit more—well, more."

Neval shrugged. "It seemed bigger when we were kids, I 'spose."

Rowan nodded slowly, then turned his sharp gaze back to Neval.

"I heard what happened, Neval."

"Y-you did?" Panic welled in Neval's chest and he frantically searched Rowan's eyes for some clue of his reaction. His friend's brow remained furrowed, eyes sharp on Neval.

"Yeah, and I know you didn't mean for it to 'appen."

"I didn't," Neval said hurriedly, relief flooding through him. "I swear it was an accident."

Rowan nodded solemnly. "You should know though, Neval, he deserved it—surely as anyone."

"He deserved—" Confusion quickly gave way to realization as Neval saw Rowan's jaw tighten. "You mean the Bellator."

"Tegan told me everything. And truly, Neval, I thank you." He clapped a hand on Neval's shoulder. "If you hadn't been there—" He swallowed hard. "Well, I'm just glad you were and that you had the courage to act. Not many would, you know. I'm proud to call you my brother."

A sour taste burned in the back of Neval's mouth and he felt physically ill, barely getting out, "O-of course, I mean it was *Tegan*."

Rowan nodded, rubbing a hand along the back of his neck. "Well, for what it's worth, I'm sorry. You two wouldn't even have been there if I hadn't been off . . . well, doesn't matter what I was doing. I'm sorry." He glanced nervously up at him and, to Neval's horror, he realized Rowan felt *guilty*. The knife in his gut twisted deeper.

"It's fine Rowan, really."

Rowan shrugged. "Could have been a lot worse, I suppose. Anyway, what are we going to do about you, then?"

Neval swallowed. "Are they still searching for me?"

"They are, but they don't know who they're searching for— just a vague description, tall, gangly teenage boy with floppy brown hair and below average looks."

Rowan grinned and Neval snorted, though the amusement was short-lived.

"It won't be long then. Some villager's sure to rat me out. I'm sure the celebration party's already in the works."

Rowan eyed him curiously, an odd smile tugging at the corner of his mouth. "I wouldn't be so sure of that if I were you."

That took Neval aback. "What, why? I'm sure they're all thrilled to be rid of me. The town drunk's good-for-nothing son finally getting what he deserves."

"Actually, Neval, you've become something of a hero in the village. A hero only in whispers and gossip, but a hero nonetheless."

Neval stared at him, brows raised, waiting for the punchline. He'd long accepted Rowan's jokes and jabs at his expense, but this was going a bit too far.

"Be serious, Rowan. I've got to get out of here."

"I *am* serious, Neval, and I'm not so sure you do." Something glittered in Rowan's eyes and he leaned forward. Though it was just the two of them, he murmured, "Something's changing, Neval. This is different, this is —" He paused, searching for the right word, before settling on, "You've sparked something, Neval. Something this village has been needing for a very long time. Everyone's talkin' about what you did and it's the first time since — Well, I haven't seen this type of anger, determination, and hope since my old Da was around."

Neval stared at him, registering in an instant the pain, anger, and finally . . . *hope* that flashed across Rowan's face. And he couldn't help catching a bit of it, just enough that the stone in the pit of his stomach lightened by a fraction. He wanted to believe that Rowan was right. He wanted to hope that their lives might be better, that this village, despite its cruelty, might be worth saving. If nothing else, he wanted that for Rowan and Tegan. They deserved it.

Then a thought hit him and he narrowed his eyes at his friend. "So, what exactly *were* you doing?"

Rowan shrugged, but his eyes danced mischievously. "Oh, nothing. Had a good long talk with some . . . friends at the tavern. Let's just say you're not the only one ready to show the Bellatorio what's what. Turns out maybe I'm not so different from my old Da after all."

Though his words were light, Neval could see the emotion gleaming in Rowan's eyes. And though his words sent a pit hurtling into his stomach, Neval ached for his friend, his brother. Rowan had always worshipped his father. The two had been close, and after his death Rowan had taken to wearing his clothes, bringing his father up in every conversation, and following the trade his father had always wanted for him. Everything Rowan did was a tribute to his hero.

Neval squeezed his friend's shoulder. "I know you miss your Da — foreign as the concept is to me," Neval added wryly. "But I hope you know, he'd be really proud of you — with your trade, and . . . and everything."

Rowan shrugged, but Neval saw his throat bob several times. He squeezed his shoulder again.

"Thanks, Neval," Rowan said, voice colored by a slight rasp. "I wish he'd gotten to know you, to see who you've become. He'd be proud of you, too."

Neval could only nod. More than anything, he wanted to believe that Rowan was right, that a bunch of upland villagers mattered in the grand scheme of this screwed up world. But could they actually *do* something? Actually stand up against the might of the Bellatorio and the Marian Empire? Rowan seemed to think so. But then again, Rowan was hardly the most level-headed of schemers. Neval's thoughts quickly flashed to Tegan, wondering what she thought of all this, but had to blink away the sudden image of her moonlit face staring up at him. That was *not* what he needed just then.

"I don't know if this is for me, though, Rowan. Should we really be gettin' mixed up in all this?"

Disappointment flashed across Rowan's face and Neval felt the rock settle deeper in his stomach.

"I understand, Neval. It's a lot to ask. Even so, there's a meetin' later tonight. Gregor's letting us use his back room. At the very least, you should come. People will want to hear from you, hear what happened."

Neval snorted. "Since when did anyone in Ceffí want anything to do with me, Rowan?"

Rowan's gaze never strayed from his. "Since you gave us the most hope we've had in a very long time."

Neval could only stare back at him. And before he could say anything, Rowan clapped him on the shoulder.

"At least think about it. Come back home and think it over."

Neval nodded, not trusting himself to speak as Rowan pushed his way back through the underbrush. Neval was about to shimmy himself back into the cave when Rowan suddenly stopped and turned slightly.

"By the way, Tegan hasn't been here lately, has she?"

Neval's stomach dropped precariously at the name, but managed to get out, "N-no, haven't seen her. Why?"

Rowan waved his hand flippantly. "It's nothing. She's just been acting oddly since everything happened is all."

"I mean, that's to be expected, right?" Neval said hurriedly. He could feel the truth burning in his face.

"Yeah, I 'spose you're right."

Rowan turned then and continued through the underbrush as Neval stood there, frozen to the spot and wondering how on earth he was going to make this right. The growling of his stomach interrupted his thoughts and he suddenly realized he had a more immediate need to return to the village. He had exactly zero supplies and whether he would continue on to Karthaíla or remain hidden up in this cave for the rest of his life, he'd be needing some food. So with leaden legs dragging through the underbrush, he slowly made his way west of the village, to the house he had sworn he'd never return to again.

CHAPTER

EIGHT

Neval eased open the door to the farm shack, praying the hinges didn't squeak as he slipped inside. He blinked against the dim light, only to find the inside in surprisingly good order. The table was right side up, the chairs pushed in and even a small fire glowed in the hearth. It almost looked like a home, Neval thought wryly.

"'Bout time you showed up."

Neval spun to find a figure perched on the end of the bed. The man stood up and took a hesitant step toward him, bringing him more solidly into the full light of the fire. It was definitely his father, but Neval stared in confusion at his stubble-free face and surprisingly clear eyes. He hadn't seen him this way since —

"I heard what happened," his father said in a gravely voice. "In the village. Thought you might come here. Figured I'd clean up . . . just in case."

Neval said nothing, but kept his distance as he eyed the man suspiciously. Erik Brennan's still slightly bloodshot eyes considered him with equal wariness. "I thought you might —"

The sound of hoofbeats approaching the shack cut him off and Neval started in alarm.

They're coming for me.

He spun from side to side, searching for something, anything, he might use as a weapon. Then suddenly his father was before him, hands gripping his shoulder in a viselike grip.

"Leave it to me, Neval. I'll handle this."

Neval gaped at him, not daring to believe that this was the same man who'd run away from every fight in his life, who'd all but abandoned his son after his wife's death. This couldn't possibly be him.

And yet his father pushed open the shack door and strode out to meet the half dozen Bellators that swiftly filled the farmyard, their horses side-stepping and chomping at their bits.

"H-how can I be helpin' you fine gentlemen?" His father asked, pointedly ignoring the one female Bellator in their midst. Neval groaned internally.

The crowd of Bellators said nothing, but parted ways as a powerful black stallion broke through. Its rider wore the red plumed helmet of a Millus over dark hair shot through with silver. His steely gray eyes surveyed the humble farm and shack. Neval remained in the doorway, unable to meet the man's eyes, even as he felt their probing glare.

"I'm Millus Gaius Flavius," the man replied in a low voice, rough as sandpaper. "And I'm here to investigate the murder of one of my Bellators, stationed here under the command of Centus Gregori. Where were you and your household between sunset and midnight last night?"

A lump caught in Neval's throat and he struggled to swallow, forcing air through his nose as his heart hammered in his ears. But his father remained cool, disinterested. He merely shrugged, saying, "It's just my boy and I here and we haven't been into town since yesterday."

Millus Flavius's eyes flashed to Neval, scanning him carefully. Neval forced himself to meet his eyes, smoothing his face into a mask of innocent curiosity.

"Really?" Flavius asked. "Your boy didn't go to school today? He certainly looks of an age."

Neval swallowed the rising panic in his chest but couldn't stop his eyes from shooting to his father, who merely shrugged.

"We're farmers. The sowin' comes first," he said, gesturing

toward the newly plowed field. "Besides, my son is none too good with schoolin.' Most days it's a torment to go. If you ask the schoolmaster, he'll tell you as much."

Embarrassment burned Neval's face as he heard a few Bellators snort in derision. But Millus Flavius said nothing, merely continued surveying Neval thoughtfully.

"I already spoke to the schoolmaster. He's the one who suggested we pay you a visit."

Cold fury rippled through Neval and he scrambled at the last moment to smooth it from his face. But it was too late.

Flavius had seen it.

His quick eyes narrowed slightly, registering in an instant all Neval's pent up fury and hatred aimed at everyone and everything that had made his life a living hell for the last sixteen years.

Flavius cocked his head thoughtfully before dismounting and striding toward Neval.

Neval didn't move, gluing himself to the spot even as every muscle in his body itched to run, to flee from this very clear, very present threat.

Finally, Flavius stood before him, a whole head taller than him, eyes boring down into his. They weren't cruel eyes, but they were calculating and the steel laced through them told Neval that this was a man who would not play games when it came to fulfilling his duty. Which, in that moment, meant putting Neval behind bars. Neval could only hope the Millus did not yet realize that fact.

"I have a son about your age."

Neval blinked in surprise.

"S—sir?"

"He's never cared much for school, either. Too busy drawing or painting, or some other such nonsense. Absolutely bedeviled his schoolmasters, one and all."

"Maybe he needs the escape."

Neval clamped his mouth shut, grinding his teeth as his heart thudded in his chest. Beside him, his father stiffened noticeably. What exactly had possessed him to talk back to a Millus?

But something like a smile tugged at the corner of Flavius' mouth.

"Hmm," he murmured, considering. "That may be." Then he asked, "Have you ever been outside your village, boy?"

Startled once more, Neval could only shake his head.

Flavius nodded thoughtfully, as if expecting this answer. "Well, it's an enormous world, as I'm sure you've been told. A world filled with its own share of injustice and suffering." Flavius paused, taking in their surroundings, the crumbling shack and barren fields. Neval felt his cheeks burn.

"Sometimes," Flavius continued, "when our world is very small, we start to think that our suffering is somehow unique, that our difficulties arise not from the same struggle as everyone else, but that we are oppressed, deprived of opportunity by those who seem to have already succeeded."

Neval said nothing, unsure where this was all going.

"In such cases, one might be tempted to take matters into their own hands, even taking up arms against those we deem to have harmed us. Do you understand what I'm saying, son?"

"S-sir?" Neval stammered. "I surely know nothing about that."

Flavius cocked his head, surveying Neval silently, before nodding.

"Very good, then. See that it remains that way. Because I'll tell you now, son. That wider world you've never been to, it has no patience for those who throw themselves upon the cogs of its inexorable machine. It will merely chew you up and spit you out again. Trust me, I have seen it." Something flashed in Flavius's eyes then, making Neval wonder exactly what this man had seen in his years spent leading armies and suppressing rebellion. But he wasn't done.

"I am charged with keeping order within that system, such as it is," Flavius continued. "And I will not hesitate to fulfill my duty as such. Construction of the Karthaíla Dam will move forward as scheduled. Nothing and *no one* will stop it. Do you understand?"

Neval swallowed, then nodded in a jerking motion.

And with that, Flavius turned and mounted his black stallion. Signaling for the others, they turned and trotted back down the road, aiming no doubt for the other farmhouses that dotted Ceffi's perimeter.

Neval couldn't move, remaining frozen to the spot even as his father came up behind him and steered him back inside the house. But Neval refused to move past the doorway.

"You knew they'd come," Neval said slowly, careful to keep his distance still.

His father shrugged, running a hand roughly across the back of his neck.

"I figured they might come here, wanted to clean up so the place looked a bit more . . . respectable."

Neval stared at him in disbelief, fingers reaching instinctively for the shard of his mother's ceramic vase that remained in his pocket.

"I never asked for you to do anything."

His father nodded solemnly, clearly expecting this. "I know you didn't. You never do. Not that I've given you any reason to, mind. I'm no fool. I know what . . . what you must think of me."

Neval said nothing, staring at his father in disbelief. This was by far the most clear-headed he'd been in years, and he had no clue how to react.

"But I just want you to know, Neval. That I — well, I'm proud of you. For whatever that's worth, which I suspect is little. And if you need help with what's comin', well, I'd be glad to lend a hand, such as it is." He stretched out his hands, warped from the arthritis that had plagued him since he was a young man, and barked a humorless laugh, thick with despair and laced with that ever-present thread of bitterness. That was a laugh Neval was all-too familiar with, and it made Neval stiffen at once. "I don't need or want anything from you, old man. Go back to your mogda and try to forget the years of torment you put me through in this house. For I surely won't, and neither will *she*."

At his words, something shattered in his father's face and Neval watched as he slowly sagged back onto the bed.

Good, he thought. But there was no venom in it. He was simply too tired. Neval turned away from that hollowed out face and began searching the room for any scraps of food he might scavenge away. He had to get out of there, right now.

"In the barrel by the fire," said the rasping voice from behind him. And Neval paused, insanely tempted to ignore the suggestion out of pure spite.

"I picked up a few things at the market, in case you came and needed something." Neval swallowed hard before deciding he couldn't afford to turn down free food, no matter its source. Inside the barrel, Neval found two loaves of bread and a chunk of cheese. He glanced back in surprise at his father, who still sat on the bed facing the wall. This was more than his father had provided in years.

"It's not much," his father whispered. "But it's yours. I owe you that much."

Neval gritted his teeth against the sudden thread of pity that coursed through him.

This changed nothing, he reminded himself, erasing none of his father's failings or the torment that resulted from them. It was just bread and cheese. It meant nothing.

And with that thought, Neval scooped up the food and tossed it in his knapsack before turning toward the door. He had to get out of there before he was tempted to forgive any more of this broken man's failings. This place was rotten to the core, and that poison would eat away at him too if he stayed.

Something had to be done.

But if Millus Flavius was right, things weren't any better outside of Ceffi. No, the corruption in these lands ran too deep for any healer. There was only one way to be rid of a rot that cut to the core.

It had to be carved out.

NINE

Neval pushed his way carefully through the door to the blacksmith's shop and blinked against the gloom coating the interior. Despite the open door, the musty smell of old leather and sweat still lingered. But the indistinct murmur of voices drew him in, and he slowly made his way to the backroom.

He paused when he reached the door. What was he doing? Consorting with would-be rebels? This was lunacy at its finest. But inside churned that same impatience that had driven him from his father's house, the desire to do something — anything. The Bellatorio had tormented their village for long enough and he was finally angry enough to do something about it. He pushed open the door.

The creek of unoiled hinges drew every eye within the gathered assembly and Neval met each face in turn. He knew all of them, of course. Most of them were young men — out of the schoolhouse, but still in their apprenticeships, like Rowan. Neval hesitated at the entryway, suddenly unsure whether to stay or go. But the nearest one — Beramy, the baker's son — suddenly stood from his chair and gestured to it.

Neval gaped at him, unable to believe what he was seeing. He had never in his life, not once, been offered a seat by a villager. All around the room, eyes fell on him, and murmured words of appreciation floated toward him.

"Killed him dead."

"First strike."

"Sent 'em a message."

"Got the entire village behind him."

He stood there for another minute, even as the appreciative stares changed to ones of confusion.

This was *not* who he was.

"Neval!" came a call from the front of the room and Neval suddenly registered Rowan's bulk striding toward him. He pulled him into a bone-crushing embrace he hadn't the wherewithal to return and clapped him on the back. Behind him, Neval could just make out Tegan's honey colored head bent low as she furiously scribbled onto a piece of parchment laid out at the head table. From the looks of it, she was the lone female in the room. Neval hastily looked away, letting Rowan steer him into Beramy's proffered chair.

His legs folded at once, and he was suddenly seated next to the other young men, each offering hesitant smiles or a small word of congratulations. Neval barely managed a small nod in return, his brain still spinning in shock. But Rowan soon drew everyone's attention forward.

"All right Gents, I think we know why we're all here."

"Stop the dam!" cried one voice from the back.

"Drive those bastards out!" shouted another.

Rowan held up a hand for quiet, but nodded somberly in agreement. "Ay lads, that's right. We've all grown used to havin' stinkin' red cloaks about, payin' their thievin' taxes, and feelin' the weight of their boots on our necks. But this time they've gone too far. Just ask my best friend Neval here." He gestured in Neval's direction and suddenly all eyes were again on him. Neval resisted the urge to sink lower into his chair.

"When one of those bastards had the gall to attack my betrothed, many a man would have turned a blind eye or suddenly found another alley to stroll down. But not my best friend, my brother — not Neval Brennan."

Guilt curdled in Neval's stomach as flashes of the dead Bellator and Tegan's tear-stained face gazed up at him. He was suddenly very concerned he might be sick.

He needn't have said anything though, for cries of agreement echoed around the room.

"Done takin' it!"

"Showed that bastard what's what!"

Rowan allowed the shouts to continue for another minute and Neval glanced nervously at the door, sure whoever passed outside must have heard their cries. Then Rowan held up a hand and the voices settled.

"What we need," he declared, "is a plan. A way of showin' the Marians that we're not to be trifled with and we certainly won't accept mistreatment."

With a dramatic flourish, Rowan unfurled a map onto the table before him and the young men all gathered around eagerly. Even Neval strained his neck to see.

"The Bellatori Camp," Rowan pronounced, pausing on each syllable for effect. "Scouted it this morning. It's less than a mile outside Ceffí, just beside the dam's future construction site. They've only just started setting it up so there are no real fortifications yet. I say it's high time we paid it a visit, a bit of a *welcomin'* party if you like."

Harsh chuckles echoed around the room and Neval looked between each of their faces. They were all young, some even younger than him, and yet the same look of eagerness lit up each of their faces. Raised on tales of the Ceffí rebels' last stand, they'd been waiting a long time for their chance at revenge.

"We'll strike at night," Rowan declared. "Hit the encampment just south of the construction site. We'll sneak up when they're all in their beds and cut 'em down before they know what's happened."

Hit the encampment? A fortified position?

Neval didn't like the sound of that, not one bit. But Rowan was already moving on to the details of the plan, his finger dancing over the rough-hewn lines of his homemade map as his voice rose and fell like a storyteller's, painting a picture of victory and revenge. But all Neval could see was the dead Bellator lying in a pool of blood in the street.

Then the picture changed.

In his mind, the prone figure became Rowan. Tegan's tear-streaked face gazed up at him from where she kneeled, hands clawing at Rowan's body, her eyes filled with accusation. Neval shuddered, trying to clear the image from his mind, but still it persisted. He fought down the wave of nausea that followed.

Neval glanced over to where Tegan had sat, hoping desperately for a rational ally amidst this insanity. But she was gone. Her quills and parchments had disappeared and the back door was still somewhat ajar.

Odd.

But before he could think on her strange disappearance more, cheers of excitement and determination signaled the meeting was at an end. Rowan shook each hand as the young men slipped out the door, murmuring words of thanks and encouragement, and even slapping a few on the back as they went.

"So, what did you think?" Rowan asked, face lit up and eager. "Think we have what it takes to give those red cloaks a good poundin'?"

Neval stared at him in disbelief.

"What did I think? Rowan, you're all going to get yourselves killed!"

The smile vanished from Rowan's face as quickly as it had come and he stood to his full height, a full head above Neval. He crossed his arms over his broad chest until the fabric strained. "Well, it's risky, obviously. But we ain't gonna get nowhere if we're not willin' to accept some risk."

Neval shook his head. "I'm not talking about avoiding all risk, just those plans with exactly zero chance of succeeding."

Rowan scowled at him.

"You don't know that."

"Yes, yes I do."

Rowan said nothing, but his eyes narrowed, and he clenched his jaw. Neval gaped at him. Was he really this dense? Was his hate and fury really so great that he couldn't see the absolute folly of this plan?

"Rowan," he began slowly. "I know you want to do this for your father, but there has to be a better—"

"You don't know anything, Neval." Rowan spat. "Is that really all you care about, then? Saving your own skin? Running away and making a better life for yourself, the rest of us be damned?"

Neval blinked in surprise.

"Yeah," Rowan said. "T told me what your plans were the other night. I thought maybe, just maybe, after everything that's happened, you might for once in your life grow a spine and stand up for yourself. But I guess not."

A roaring echoed in Neval's ears, and before he realized what he was doing, he stepped forward and gave Rowan a rough shove. Rowan didn't go far, but he staggered back, more out of surprise than anything. Still, a pool of satisfaction curdled in Neval's gut. It didn't last long, as Rowan's face quickly morphed from surprise to fury. He rounded on him and shoved Neval roughly.

Neval saw it coming, but as he tried to dodge, his foot caught on a chair leg and he stumbled backwards, landing squarely on his behind.

"What on earth is going on here?" A voice demanded. Rowan and Neval both looked up sheepishly to find Tegan standing, arms crossed, in the doorway.

Humiliation burned in Neval's cheeks, and he quickly scrambled to his feet, trying to dust himself off as inconspicuously as possible.

"It's nothing," he murmured, barely meeting her concerned eyes. But he caught the change as her face suddenly paled and she looked between him and Rowan.

"You didn't — You're not fighting about — "

Her voice cut off and in horror, Neval suddenly realized how this must look. He opened his mouth to reassure her but came up short, not wanting to give anything away either.

"It's nothing, T," Rowan finally said, shrugging. "Just a slight tactical disagreement."

"Tactical?" Tegan asked dubiously, looking between the two warily. "You were brawling over tactics?"

Rowan nodded. "You see, Neval here came to the meeting tonight and decided since he's now the master of anti-Bellatorio insurgency, that we're all off our heads and gonna get ourselves killed."

Neval scowled at the sarcasm and opened his mouth to reply, when Tegan suddenly interjected.

"You should listen to him, Rowan. If you won't talk to me about it, at least let your friend weigh in. Neval's a fresh pair of eyes and he's smarter than you give him credit for," she said fiercely.

Neval felt warmth flood his chest, but it faded quickly as Rowan shot a glance of confusion between the two of them. "I'm not sayin' he ain't smart, just that he can't come in here and change up all our plans on the first visit."

"Well, if they're bad plans—"

"They're *not* bad plans! I worked really hard on them, Tegan." Hurt colored Rowan's voice and he glanced warily at Neval and then back to Tegan, brow furrowing.

Neval could hear his heart thudding in his ears and sweat prickled on the back of his neck. This was *not* good. He could feel Tegan's presence like a branding iron mere inches from his skin and he struggled to keep his mind focused. Why did she keep defending him? She was bound to make Rowan suspicious. She and Rowan were still arguing back and forth when Neval couldn't take it any longer.

"I-I changed my mind," he blurted, watching as two pairs of wide eyes turned to stare at him in disbelief. "I-I've thought it over and I think it's worth a shot. I—I'd like to help."

Barely missing a beat, Rowan crowed in delight, clapping Neval on the back. "I knew we could count on you, brother. We'll show those slimy bastards what's what. Mark my words."

Tegan's eyes tightened and her brow furrowed even deeper. "Neval, I thought you said it wasn't a good idea."

"I-I've changed my mind," Neval said, ignoring how the way she said his name sent goosebumps coursing down his body.

"Neval, you don't have to—"

"C'mon, give it a rest, T," Rowan barked, throwing an arm around her shoulder and giving her a squeeze. "He said he's changed his mind. Let him be."

Tegan pursed her lips. "I just worry—"

Rowan silenced her by planting a massive kiss on her lips. And when he pulled away, Tegan was blushing scarlet, glancing between Neval and Rowan.

"I know you do, love. But never worry. Neval and I will take good care of each other, won't we, Neval?"

Personally, Neval thought he might be sick, but carefully kept his face neutral as he gave a sharp nod. Tegan said nothing.

"Right then," Rowan announced, turning to gather up the remaining papers. "That settles things. In the meantime, we're looking for a place to stash some extra weapons. We're hoping for a good turnout from lads in the surrounding villages, but can't be sure how many will show. Is your root cellar still empty? I know you mentioned it had flooded last week."

Neval could barely hear him over the roaring in his ears, but he nodded numbly.

"Perfect. Come by the shop tomorrow and we'll load everything up in the wagon to take 'em over. As for the raid, we'll meet at your farm at dusk next Saturday. So don't be late. We got some red cloaks to skewer." Laughing at his own joke, Rowan pushed through the door to the main blacksmith's shop.

Quickly, Tegan turned toward Neval. In the soft candlelight of the back room, her cheeks glistened and her eyes glowed brightly with concern. She reached out a hand toward him and blood roared in his ears.

"Neval, I—"

Neval pushed past her, heading for the door. He couldn't do this. He wasn't this person. And yet every second he remained alone with her, he risked turning into someone he didn't even recognize. Neval pushed through the door to the main blacksmith's shop, trying to forget the look of hurt that flashed across Tegan's face as the door swung shut behind him. But the hollow-

ness in his stomach was not so easily ignored and followed him far
out into the night.

CHAPTER

TEN

The dark lay heavily all around them, the moonless sky a thick blanket that threatened to suffocate the young men who creeped silently toward the Bellatori camp—its single point of light a beacon in the dark. The young men had come from the surrounding villages, answering the Crimson Quill's covert call that had spread in hushed whispers over tavern ale and candlelight. Though still calling their plan foolish, Tegan had worked double time this past week, marshaling every contact she had from distributing her secret writings to give them the best chance of success. Neval could only hope it would be enough. He kept close to Rowan, fingers curled tightly around the knife at his hip, the notches in its hilt pressing painfully into his palm.

This is a terrible idea, the voice in the back of his head chanted.

Neval swallowed, silencing the voice with a glance at Rowan. Even in the dark, he could see the gleam of excitement in his eyes. No, there'd be no stopping him. And if his best friend was sneaking off into almost certain death, well, what kind of person was he if he didn't do everything he could to protect him?

Even if it means we both end up dead?

Neval swallowed. *Even then.*

At his side, Rowan raised a hand for the group to halt and they all dropped to one knee. Neval's heart thudded in his chest as he watched the slow bobbing of a torch behind the makeshift fortifications ahead—the changing of the guard.

With a quick twist of his wrist, Rowan signaled and the men dispersed into their positions encircling the camp. Neval kept to Rowan's side as they darted in between the rows of palisades, making their way toward the still smoldering campfire between the nearest circle of tents.

Not quite believing they'd made it inside, Neval's stomach churned with nerves and even a hint of excitement. Could they actually pull this off?

Pulling one of their many makeshift torches from his back, Neval kneeled beside the embers of the campfire. But just as he lightly blew on the fading flames, motion to his right made him freeze.

The dark shape he'd at first taken for a pile of saddlebags slowly shifted and rolled.

From across the fire pit, Rowan's eyes widened and he jerked his head toward the shape, motioning with his knife in encouragement.

Neval opened his mouth but no words came out and he felt the blood slowly drain from his face. As he turned back to stare in horror at the shape, one sleepy eye and then another opened, blinking at him in brow furrowing confusion. Neval willed his legs to move, but he'd just as soon wrench tree trunks from their hold. In his mind's eye he saw another Bellator's face, drained of life, mouth opened in a silent scream.

The bundled man before him blinked furiously, and was moving to sit up, when a flash of movement to the side drew both their stares. In an instant, Rowan was on top of him, hand pressed hard against the man's mouth, muffling his strangled cries. And with a practiced air from years spent slaughtering his mother's pigs, Rowan slashed the blade across the man's throat.

Neval stared in horror as blood gushed onto the ground and the man's violent jerking slowed. Chest heaving, Rowan turned back and leveled Neval with an icy glare.

You've killed before, that look asked. *Why not now?*

Neval swallowed, turning back to the glowing embers. His

stomach churned as he fought to wrangle control of his pounding pulse.

In an instant, Rowan was behind him, fanning a tiny flame until it just barely took hold of their makeshift torches. They were both grinning at each other in delight when a cry of alarm from across the camp sent them both scrambling to their feet.

From across the camp, shouts echoed and shadowed forms burst from tents as tongues of flame licked higher into the air. Nearby, Neval heard the stirring of heavy bodies and he glanced in panic at Rowan.

"Now!" Rowan cried and he sprung toward the nearest tent, slashing his brazen torch across its entrance with a feral scream. The flames caught immediately on the oiled canvas and Rowan darted between tents with a sadistic ferocity, reveling in the surge of fire in his wake.

"What are you waiting for, Neval? This is it!"

But Neval stood rooted in place, gaping as the groggy murmurs from inside the tents soon turned into shouts of alarm and then screams of pain and fear.

"I—I can't do this."

"What?" Rowan's voice was incredulous. He turned to stare at Neval, who could see barely contained anger throbbing beneath the surface.

"I just — " The words caught in his throat as he stared in horror at the burly shape emerging from a tent just behind Rowan, the glint of steel clutched in one meaty fist.

"Rowan MOVE!"

Rowan's mouth gaped at him as he slowly, *too* slowly, turned toward the looming threat. He didn't have time to speak as Neval dashed forward, and one hand gripping his shirt front, dragged him bodily back in the direction they'd come. The massive Bellator lurched toward them, one swing of his sword slicing within inches of Rowan's back, but they were already running.

"Neval, the mission!" Rowan cried, even as he conceded to be dragged back toward the palisades.

"We. Have. To. Move." Neval spat out between ragged breaths, his legs moving faster than they'd ever moved before. Turns out he may not have been much of a rebel, but he certainly knew how to run.

Only this time, it was too little too late.

From all sides, Bellators sprang from their tents, drawn by the commotion and shouts of pain. Some ran for water and others to drag their burning comrades from their tents. But many, far too many, seized weapons and rounded on the trespassers in their midst. Neval darted and weaved between tents, toppling weapon racks and kicking up burning embers, using every trick he knew from a life spent on the run. And it worked.

In the chaos of the moment, the Bellators didn't know which way to turn. But with every second that passed, Neval could feel Rowan slowing, his massive frame better suited to smelting weaponry than sprinting for his life.

Come on, Neval thought. *Just a few more yards.*

He could see a gap in the palisades just ahead of them, one of many that dotted the makeshift fortifications. But he was forced to drag them along a route tangential to it, weaving a course that hid his ultimate aim from their furious pursuers.

Their friends weren't so lucky. From the corner of his eye, Neval could see their fellow rebels being forced into corners, bravely wielding whatever weapons they had at hand, and one after another falling to Bellatori steel. Neval resisted the urge to clamp a hand over his ears as their choked screams intermingled with those of the still-burning Bellators.

Neval forced his gaze away, refusing to slow their pace as he dragged the staggering Rowan ever forward. But even as they ran, Neval could feel the twisting path he took between the tents narrowing, the canvas growing closer and closer together until they were squeezing between them. But Neval never took his eyes off that gap in the palisades, determined to reach it no matter what.

And it *was* growing nearer. Neval allowed the flicker of hope to grow in his chest. They could make it. They *would* make it.

But as they rounded the last corner of tents, Neval and Rowan skidded to a halt as a massive figure lumbered out of the darkness before them.

"No," Neval breathed, watching as the Bellatori giant from before once again took shape. They were so close. The gap was right *there*. Neval's eyes darted around them, looking for something, anything, they could use to escape.

Rowan said nothing beside him, chest still heaving as he fought to catch his breath.

So far it was just the one Bellator, but Neval knew it was only a matter of time until they drew the attention of others.

"Filthy upland scum," the giant growled. Close enough now to distinguish his features, Neval could clearly see the rippling muscle beneath the man's bronzed skin, the dark brows that shadowed his eyes. One beefy fist grasped a meat cleaver from the butcher block at his side. Neval wondered absently what happened to the giant's massive blade.

Probably lodged inside one of our friends, he thought darkly.

Rowan swallowed loudly beside him and Neval saw him clench his fist around his own weapon, a kitchen knife that seemed woefully inadequate under the circumstances. They were no match, Neval knew, glancing down at his own dagger and the torch he still clutched in one hand.

Then Neval's eyes snapped back to the butcher block, immediately taking in its surroundings—baskets of vegetables, a cauldron on a banked fire, and the rows of carefully stacked clay pots filled to the brim with cooking oil.

Neval moved without thinking, scooping up the stone at his feet and eyes snapping to the pot at the base of the stack, just off-center — the one he knew instinctively bore the brunt of the stack's weight.

He let the stone fly.

The pot shattered and with it, the rest cascaded down to the ground, smashing to pieces and forming a river of oil that cut just in front of the giant's feet.

Neval felt a small smile of satisfaction tug at his lips as he sent his torch sailing in a graceful arc up and into the shards of crockery.

The flames erupted skyward in an instant, sending the giant staggering back with a howl as he clutched at his face.

"Let's go!" Neval cried, dragging a stunned Rowan sideways toward the gap in the palisades.

Any second now, more Bellators would descend on them, drawn by the soaring flames and the giant's howls. It was now or never. They had to get out of there.

They reached the gap and Neval easily slipped through, silently panicking as the much larger Rowan had to wedge himself through the small gap.

"Come on, come on!" Neval muttered under his breath. But with a final heave, Rowan staggered through, and Neval seized him, taking off at a dead sprint toward the forest in the distance.

The shouts behind them intensified, but Neval didn't dare look back, even as the soft whistle of arrows soared past them. They were close, *so* close.

Their breath was ragged as they finally reached the tree line, but Neval refused to stop, dragging Rowan ever forward, back toward the town.

As the minutes passed, Neval could feel them both slowing, and their heavy breathing took on a pained sound. Finally, when the lights of the burning encampment had faded into the dark behind them, Neval allowed them to slow to a walk.

For several minutes the only sound that filled the air was that of their ragged breathing, but as the minutes past even that quieted, until all that was left was a heavy silence, weighed down by all that had happened and carried only by the two that remained. Neither spoke of it, of the failed mission, or of the eager young men that now lay dead. They let it settle between them uneasily as they continued onward.

Yet when Rowan finally spoke, it wasn't what Neval expected at all.

"H-how did you know to do that?" Rowan murmured, awe filling his voice.

Neval blinked at him, confused. "Do what?"

"Where to strike the stack of pots, how to predict the direction they'd fall."

The question took Neval aback and he was silent for a moment, thinking.

"I don't know, I just *knew*. It's all angles and weight. I mean, how do you know where to strike iron? The exact angle needed to shape an axe or a sickle?"

Rowan's brow furrowed as he cocked his head over at Neval.

"I've been a blacksmith's apprentice for two years and I can barely make nails that are halfway straight. What you can do? Well, you'd be wasted as a farmer, Neval, that's for sure."

Neval stared at his friend, at a complete loss for words. This was Rowan, his friend, yes, but one who'd always teased him for his difficulty with letters and words, who'd always said it was a good thing farmers had no need of books. Something swelled in Neval's chest and he swallowed heavily, letting the silence fill the air between them as they made their way back to Ceffí.

CHAPTER

ELEVEN

Neval limped toward the farm shack, every inch of his body screaming in protest. But even worse than the pain was the replay in his mind's eye of everything that had occurred — the heat of the flames, the screams of agony, the contorted faces of the young would-be rebels as they collapsed in a heap. Those young men, the first who'd ever looked at him with anything other than disdain — all dead now. It was a minor miracle that he and Rowan had escaped.

Neval closed his eyes, shaking his head against the flood of images. All he wanted now was a warm bed and the welcome abyss of sleep.

As he pushed the door open, he was surprised to find a crackling fire in the hearth. *Odd,* he thought. His father was usually blackout drunk by this time of night.

"Neval?" The trembling voice came from the bed and he jerked his head in surprise to see none other than Tegan. She uncurled herself from the tight ball she'd been in and slowly rose to her feet. Even from the door, Neval could see the tear streaks down her face and his stomach twisted with guilt.

She ran toward him, colliding in an impact that sent waves of pain coursing down his bruised body. He didn't care.

His arms tightened around her reflexively, and she buried her face in his chest, her shoulders heaving.

73

"Shhh, it's all right," he murmured, at a loss for what else to say. She was *here*, in their filthy shack. But rather than the embarrassment that would normally course through his veins, he just felt . . . relief.

Everything would be all right now.

"W-we heard what happened back in the village. Someone saw the camp burning and then there were the screams—"

Her words choked off as she swallowed another sob.

"It's all right, I'm all right."

"A-and Rowan?"

A knife twisted in his gut, but he nodded. "Rowan's fine too. Both a bit battered and bruised, but nothing a good night's rest won't cure."

Tegan swallowed, nodding.

"I-I didn't know what to do. Couldn't go to Rowan's mother—nothing she could do but worry with all those little ones running around. Neval I—I had to tell somebody—find somebody who could help."

Neval took a hesitant step, holding Tegan at arm's length as he slowly looked around the otherwise empty room. In her face, she saw guilt and panic alike. Realization suddenly dawned.

"Tegan, where's my father?"

"N-Neval, I didn't know what to do!" Fat tears once again rolled down her cheeks. "I had to find someone who could help."

"You told my father." He said the words flatly, though disbelief coursed through every syllable. "You know what my life's like, what *he's* like. How could you get him involved?"

"I told you, Neval, I didn't know what to do." Her words sharpened defensively at his accusatory tone and she scowled up at him. "When we heard the raid had gone sideways, I knew you'd need help. A-and he's seemed . . . different, lately. And then he immediately left to go find you . . . I don't know, I just thought—"

"You *thought*? Tegan, you didn't think at all!"

Tegan jerked away from him. "*I* didn't think? Who was it that just agreed to run off on a suicide mission out of some misplaced guilt over kissing his best friend's betrothed? You think *that's* what friendship is? Agreeing with every harebrained idea someone comes up with? That's not friendship, Neval. That's not *love*."

Neval gaped at her, suddenly at a loss for words. She balled her hands into fists and scowled at him, her puffy eyes and tear-streaked face tilting up at him stubbornly.

"I just wanted to protect him, T," Neval finally breathed. "He would have done it anyway, and I couldn't let anything happen to him, especially not after . . ." He waved vaguely at the two of them, unable to voice the guilt that gnawed at him.

Tegan's lips parted slightly, as if to say something, but she pressed them firmly back together. Instead, she took his hand in both of hers and pressed it to her lips. Electricity sizzled through him, and he blinked furiously, trying to focus on the conversation at hand.

"You're a good person, Neval Brennan," Tegan whispered, her warm breath brushing against his skin. Almost without thinking, Neval took a step toward her, running a hand lightly down her arm, slowly, hesitantly.

Tegan dropped his hand and stepped toward him, lightly cupping his face with both of her hands. Her body was millimeters from his and he felt his stomach tighten. But when she looked up at him, tears glistened in her eyes and the firelight danced off her freckled nose. Both of his hands moved to her waist as if of their own accord, and she pressed herself against him, her lips moving to his ear as she cradled the back of his neck.

"I was so scared, Neval, for both of you. I—I thought I might never see you again and—" Her voice cut off in a choked sob.

Neval swallowed, trying to keep a hold of himself, focusing only on her words, and not the softness of her body against him.

"And you what?" His voice sounded rough even to his own ears, and she pulled back to stare wide eyed at him.

"And I knew," she said simply, looking him straight in the eye. Though her eyes still glistened, no more tears fell. "I made a mistake, Neval. I—I want to be with you, just you."

Her lips were so close to his that he could feel her breath tickling the light scruff of his face. He shuddered slightly, pulling her even tighter against him, burying his face in her neck, letting the smell of her hair wash over him, sinking into it.

"W-we have to tell him, Tegan." Neval whispered almost desperately. He could feel himself getting sucked in and he resisted it even as a part of him reveled in the intoxicating smell of her, letting it go straight to his head. "He has to know."

Her own breath was ragged as she replied, "We will."

Then he kissed her.

It was a deep kiss, nothing like after the attack, and the two of them fell headlong into it — into each other.

Neval dragged his lips across her jaw to her ear, exhilarated by the low moan that ripped from her. He wanted this more than he'd wanted anything. He wanted her. And suddenly everything that had occurred that night, the pain, the death, the fear, it all faded into the back of his mind. There was nothing else but Tegan.

How long had he waited for this? How many years had he loved her, his best friend and the girl he could never be with? That he could never deserve? So, as she tugged him lightly backwards toward the bed, he followed willingly. He let his guilt and fear fade into the background, happy to forget everything in favor of this one moment — the happiest he could remember being in his entire life.

HIS FATHER HAD RETURNED LATER that night, long after Tegan had left. But he'd said nothing to Neval, barely sparing him a glance before collapsing into bed. Neval didn't know what to make of it. Had he already forgotten why he'd left the house mere hours before? Neval decided it was the least of his concerns.

Yet over the weeks that followed, Neval watched his father warily as the old man seemed to take a renewed interest in their farm — cutting irrigation furrows into the land and repairing long-worn equipment. Neval didn't let himself get comfortable with this apparent change of heart. This wasn't his father's first sober bout. He knew better than to trust it.

Rather, Neval watched the road with anxious attention,

waiting for the day the Bellatorio came knocking on the farm door, looking once more for rebel sympathizers. But every day he woke to find he could still walk free.

Other changes were afoot, though. In the weeks following the failed raid on the Bellatori camp, security in the village multiplied to its most oppressive yet. Checkpoints tripled in number as villagers were waylaid and subjected to impromptu searches and seizure. The Bellatorio also took it upon themselves to raid residents' homes, making arrests in the dead of night. The attack on his encampment had incensed Centus Gregori, who offered a reward to any villager with information, all the while ordering public beatings of anyone who failed to comply with search and seizure demands.

Meanwhile, construction on the dam continued unabated, aided by the conscription of able-bodied men throughout the local villages. And with each rain that came that spring, the water levels of the river rose, flooding nearby farmland and creeping ever closer to the village.

No one was left unscathed — a point made painfully clear when Neval returned home one rainy day to find his father collapsed on his knees beside their field. Erik's haggard face was etched with numb despair as he stared at the remains of their newly sprouted field, now rotting under a foot of muddy water.

His father disappeared shortly after that.

Neval briefly considered looking for him, but reminded himself that Erik had no doubt fallen into one of his well-known drinking binges. He shouldn't have been surprised. But with no small amount of shame, Neval had to acknowledge the tiny part of him which had thought that maybe this time would be different. He'd been a fool.

Some families were quick to admit defeat, packing up what belongings they could and heading for the downland and whatever new life they might find. But more stayed, that same stubborn streak that had long defined the uplands, out in full force.

The mood in Ceffí quickly turned dark, and angry mutterings on street corners intensified. Stranger still was the response Neval himself elicited. As one of the sole survivors of the failed raid, combined with his existing reputation after Tegan's attack, everywhere he went, whispers followed. And any number of villagers who, a month prior, would sooner spit at him as look at him, now seemed in awe. Men now clapped him on the back and older women offered him baskets of baked goods since he was "so awfully thin," as their daughters giggled flirtatiously in the corner.

"I don't know what to make of it," he exclaimed to the ceiling one night. Lying on his back on a pallet before the fireplace of his shack with Tegan tucked under one arm, Neval stared upward, trying and failing to make sense of his new reality. "My whole life these folk told me I was nothin' better than scum off their boots, that I'd amount to nothing. And now suddenly I'm worth something? Why? Because I killed some people? Men I didn't even know, who'd done nothin' to me directly? I don't get it."

Tegan was quiet for a long moment, tracing some unseen design on his chest and as the minutes passed, Neval let himself be calmed by the slow methodical movement of her fingers.

"People like a story, Neval," she said finally. "Someone to root for, another to blame. It's in their nature. Everyone's so angry right now. And here you are, gone and changed your own story. No longer the peasant son of the town drunk, you're a hero, a rebel, someone to give the people hope. It takes a lot of courage to change the story of your own life."

"That's a hell of a lot of pressure," Neval grumbled. "I never wanted this, never wanted to be some sort of rebel. I just wanted acceptance — enough to get by, to be just like everyone else."

Tegan propped herself up on one arm, staring down with a bemused expression on her face. "Is that really all you wanted? Their acceptance? For as long as I've known you, Neval, you've dreamed of something bigger than this place. You've dreamed of the city, of making something of yourself."

"As an architect," Neval grumbled again. "Not some sort of rebel leader."

Tegan ignored him, her eyes tightening as she lay back down beside him. "If it were me, I'd just be grateful, Neval. We don't all get the chance to change our story." These last words held a bitter edge and Neval didn't know what to say to that.

A week earlier, her parents had finally forced Tegan to leave school. While it was under the pretense that there was too much unrest for her to be out and about on her own, Tegan declared that her mother was just finally getting her way. She now spent her days on menial household chores, sewing and embroidering clothing for a trousseau she now had no intention of using.

"We have to tell him," Neval said quietly, unsurprised when Tegan stiffened at his familiar words.

"I can't," she replied. "Not yet. Not with all this unrest. And definitely not with him risking his life every night. He doesn't need any distractions and I refuse to be the reason he gets himself killed."

Neval swallowed. He knew Tegan felt guilty. After all, it was the Crimson Quill's broadsides that Rowan was distributing to the nearby villages under cover of darkness. Decrying Marian abuses, they were also filled with coded messages mustering support for their cause.

Neval had wondered if she would stop writing after the botched attack on the Bellatori Camp. But it seemed she couldn't quite give it up—the one thing in her life that seemed to give her purpose and meaning amongst days filled with embroidery and minding her parent's General Store. He could understand that. So, he helped her with them, listening as she read aloud reports of all the Bellatorio had done in Ceffí and elsewhere. He offered suggestions here and there, turns of phrase that would please the ear and stir the soul as they were read aloud in taverns all over the region.

For his part, Rowan was so filled with shame over the failed raid that he'd jumped at any opportunity to serve the cause and redeem himself. Ceffí and the surrounding villages were still in mourning over the deaths of so many of their young men, and Rowan, as their leader, now took the brunt of their ire. Rowan could go nowhere without sidelong glances and Laoise, the baker's wife, had spat directly in his face at the market just the other day. Rowan had said nothing, simply stood rigid as a pillar and taken every furious word. Laoise's son Beramy had not survived the raid.

Their places ironically reversed, Neval could feel nothing but sympathy for his friend. He knew all too well what being the town pariah felt like and couldn't blame Rowan for doing everything he could to change that fact.

"It's his choice, T, but he deserves to know the truth. And I can't keep lying to him."

It was well-worn ground, an argument they circled back to just about every day. Neval decided to drop it, just as he always did. He silenced the nagging voice in the back of his mind, the one that whispered *betrayal* in quiet moments when he was tempted to happiness.

"Speaking of which, there's supposed to be a meeting tonight." Tegan said, eyes searching his. "You think you'll go?"

Though her voice was even, Neval heard the whisper of hope in her words, and he tried to fight the pang of jealousy that coursed through his chest. With as much as she worried about Rowan, Neval knew she liked the idea of the two of them sticking together, taking care of each other. Neval would like it too if not for the gnawing guilt that sent waves of nausea through him every time he saw his best friend — the man whose betrothed lay half-dressed beside him. Neval swallowed.

"I'm not sure."

Tegan nodded, unable to hide the disappointment on her face.

The pang of jealousy hit him again and the nagging voice once more asked, *Does she really care for you as she says? Or are you merely a distraction?*

For once, Neval didn't fight the question.

"What changed Tegan? Between us, I mean?"

Tegan blinked up at him, startled, and then snorted, "I mean you did save me from those Bellators. That was certainly a good start."

Neval brushed that aside with a wave of his hand, eyes fixed on hers.

"You know what I mean. We were friends for years. And it was always Rowan, never me. What changed?"

Tegan said nothing, but her fingers continued to trace lightly over his chest.

"Rowan was always the simpler choice, Neval. My parents pushed for it from the beginning. But after everything, well . . ." She paused before lifting her eyes to meet his with a fierceness he'd rarely witnessed. "Well, I suppose I reached a point where I was done living the life they'd planned for me. I looked at you, Neval, finally free and able to choose the life you wanted. And I wanted what you had, Neval. I wanted a life with you."

Neval thought about this for a while, unsure how he felt about her answer, but even less sure he wanted to press for clarification. He decided some questions were best left unanswered.

A sound from outside made Tegan sit bolt upright. Neval blinked at her, startled by her sudden movement.

"What was that?" She hissed, eyes darting around the darkened interior of the shack.

"Probably the wind blew over the wheelbarrow. Don't worry, it can't do any damage." That was one advantage of having mudlogged fields, Neval thought darkly. Nothing more for Mother Nature to destroy. The Empire had taken care of that once and for all.

"What about your father?" she asked, eyeing the door warily.

Neval waved a hand. "Off on a drinking binge, no doubt. I haven't seen him in days. Now come here."

Reluctantly, Tegan allowed herself to be tugged down to the blankets, relaxing slowly as Neval gently nuzzled her neck.

A howl of wind sent the door crashing against the wall, and Tegan screamed. Neval jumped to his feet, whirling to face whatever new threat this was. And there, standing in the doorway, was none other than his father.

TWELVE

Neval's father stood frozen in the doorway, saying nothing as Tegan scurried to gather her things and flee the suddenly stifling shack. Neval said nothing either, trying and failing to meet his father's gaze as he pulled on his shirt. He managed a quick squeeze of Tegan's hand and a reassuring smile before she slipped past his father and into the unseeing night.

His father closed the door behind her before sighing deeply, his knuckles whitening as he gripped the handle.

Neval braced himself, tensing for the anger and blows he knew would come.

But his father merely stood there, eyes closed and hand braced against the door. Neval shifted uneasily, unsure where this was all going.

"I hope you know what you're doing, Son."

Neval stiffened at the familiar term. But his father didn't move, merely continued to stand there. Neval ground his teeth before replying coldly.

"So it's *son* now, is it? As I remember, it was always more like *dimwit, oaf,* or *waste of space.* But sure, let's go with *son.*"

Again Neval waited, ready for the anger, the pain. Truth be told, he wanted it. He was angry—at the Bellatorio, at Ceffí, even the water that now sat ruining the meager crop they'd thought to harvest. No, he needed this. He needed something or *someone* he could fight. And his father was as good a target as any, better even. Because if anyone deserved Neval's anger, it was Erik Brennan.

But still his father said nothing and Neval felt his frustration bubble to the surface. So when his father unlatched the door and moved to push it open, Neval came right along after.

He barreled into his father with a force that sent the two of them staggering into the yard, collapsing in a muddy heap. Immediately, Neval rolled away, springing to his feet with the instincts of one who regularly dodged blows. He spun to face his father, ready to receive the powerful left hook he knew so well.

But his father remained on all fours, fingers digging into the muddy earth as raindrops rolled down his face like tears. He looked up at Neval with bloodshot eyes. Neval stared back, tracing the hard lines cut into his father's face by the punishing toll of exhaustion and time.

No, I will not give you my sympathy.

"Come on, Da." Neval kicked a pile of mud in his father's direction, smiled savagely as it sprayed across him. "Get up and show me what a disappointment I am, what a terrible friend I've become, a waste of good food and needed space."

His father didn't move, only lifted his face to the now pelting rain, his lips curving into a small smile as the drops rolled down his face. The sight only further infuriated Neval.

"Get up, old man! Get up and hit me! Don't I deserve it? Not that *that's* ever been a pre-requisite," Neval snarled. "But there's a first time for everything."

Slowly, his father climbed to his feet, joints creaking, and Neval shoved aside the twist of guilt in his gut.

"I'm done with that, Son. No more."

Neval gaped at him, shock warring with the most savage rage he'd every felt. Why couldn't his father just this once give him what he wanted, what he *needed?*

Neval spun on his heel, howling in frustration, and kicked an old cracked bucket far out into the field. Lightning immediately erupted from his foot and Neval's cry turned into one of genuine pain as he limped back toward the house. He collapsed against the wall, burying his face in his hands as he gritted his teeth against the pain in his foot.

"Why, Da? Why couldn't you be better?" He muttered the words to himself, neither asking for nor expecting a response. Instead, he glanced up to find his father sagging against the shack wall, staring off into the distance. Neither father nor son said anything for a long while until gradually the pain in Neval's foot began to fade. Finally, his father turned to face him.

"I won't betray your secret, Son. But you know as well as I what'll happen if folk learn what you've done. They respect you now, respect what you're tryin' to do. But an engagement is a sacred thing, blessed by Pneumos, and folk will not think well of anyone seekin' to break that bond."

Neval swallowed. He didn't need to be told of the risk in what he and Tegan were doing. But he couldn't give her up, not the girl he'd pined for all these years. The one who'd never chosen him, but finally had.

"I love her."

His father nodded, said nothing, and the two of them stood together, staring out at their ruined fields.

"I tried, you know, years ago."

Neval blinked in surprise before turning to stare at him. Were they really talking about this? After all this time?

"After your mother . . . well I tried to hold on, I truly did. But season after season, year after year, it was always the same. If not the drought, then storms, and if not the weather, then locusts. It never ends, and it never will."

Neval stared wide-eyed at him. It had been years since he'd heard him mention his mother, years since he'd been sober enough to have any sort of conversation at all.

"This land," Erik murmured, gesturing out at their ruined farm. "This life . . . it'll work you to the bone only to break your heart. And if it doesn't, if you do manage to survive, eking a living out of unwilling dirt, then somethin' like the Empire comes around to finish the job."

Erik swallowed audibly, a muscle tensing in his jaw as he stared straight ahead, unable to meet Neval's curious gaze. "Eventually lad, I just gave up. It isna' right nor good and I pray Pneumos has mercy on me for the mess I've made of my life, of our lives."

Neval didn't know what to say to that, what words to offer after all these years of misery — years spent hating the man beside him for his weakness, for his inability to be the father he'd needed. And Neval tried, dug deep, looking for the forgiveness he knew his father wanted.

"Neval, you have a chance. Get out, now. Go to the city like I know you've planned. Become a builder or whatever it is I've seen you scribblin' away at. Just leave this land and its curses behind."

Neval swallowed, emotions roaring within him. What he would have given to hear his father speak this way, just a few weeks earlier. And here he was, giving him permission to do what he'd always dreamed of, become the person he'd always wanted to be.

As he stared up at his father, at the weary lines cut deep into his face, the bloodshot eyes beneath sagging lids, he could see in flesh and bone what this life had cost him.

What the Empire cost him.

The thought flashed across his mind before he could stop it and along with it coursed, unbidden and unwanted, the memory of the worst day of his life.

$\sim$

THE ROOM SMELLED of sweat and decay, the air sticky from the roaring fire. His mother splayed out on the bed, eyes sunken and lips cracked, but with one hand outstretched toward him.

"Neval," her voice croaked. "Where's your father, Neval?"

Only five or six, Neval hadn't known. He'd never known. Probably in some tavern drinking away the reality of his wife's illness, forgetting the tears of a child he didn't know how to soothe and the fear that he too would any day succumb.

With a trembling hand, Neval pressed a wet cloth to his mother's brow, day and night.

"Live, Neval," was all she said, over and over again. "Live for me."

It was only when she stopped speaking and flies settled around her still open eyes that Neval stumbled out of the house, making his way shakily to each tavern in turn, looking desperately for the father he hadn't seen in days. Neval moved slowly, weak from sickness and lack of food. Evening had fallen when the door of the tavern ahead had burst open, light spilling out, along with a man heaved out into the street. The man tried to get to his feet but continued to stumble, unable to right himself. He vomited into the street as loud jeers echoed from the tavern.

Neval could only stare blankly at the swaying, filthy father he barely recognized. He reached out and placed a hand hesitantly on one arm. His father threw him off.

Tears prickled Neval's eyes and he quickly brushed them away, watching as his father once again tried to right himself.

"W-what do you want?" Erik asked, voice slurred as he starred groggily up at his only child.

"I-it's mama. S-she's not moving. I-I think she died." Neval's voice choked with tears. But his father only stared blankly back at him. Vaguely, Neval wondered if he hadn't understood. "I-I said —"

"I heard what you said," his father barked. Neval could only stare wide-eyed back at him. With sudden clarity in his voice, his father replied. "Her suffering is ended, then. We should be grateful."

Neval's mouth fell open and tears fell unbidden. His father's jaw clenched.

"She was never meant for this world, lad, for this place.*" Erik gestured wildly at the worn buildings around them, their walls lopsided and roofs threatened to cave in at any moment. Then his father's eyes met his and they narrowed at the sight of the tears streaking Neval's cheeks. "You're too like her, you know, a dreamer in a world of mud and shit. Too stupid to face the truth. And you'll suffer for it. Mark my words, you will suffer."*

His father wrenched himself to his feet then and fat tears rolled down Neval's face as he watched his father stumble away.

NEVAL HAD RESOLVED THEN and there to hate his father for the rest of his life—a task made all the easier by the years that followed, years spent begging and stealing food while his father wasted what little money they had slipping deeper and deeper into a mogda-fueled haze. Their fields lay barren, just like the life they had known.

And yet looking back, Neval could now see his father's actions for what they were—not hatred for the son who couldn't save his wife, but merely weakness and judgement clouded by grief. None of it had been Neval's fault, and it wasn't solely his father's either.

No, it was the Empire who'd done this to them. The Empire, who'd allowed a sickness to rage through the uplands without care or attention, keeping the physicians holed up in their walled downland cities, too afraid to even venture out to the hinterlands to remove the bodies that further fueled the spread.

This was their doing. And it would happen again and again and again until someone stood up to stop it—until someone had the courage to speak the truth.

We will not take it any longer.

And if that someone was really many someones, joined in common cause, well, who knew what might happen?

They would likely fail. Neval was too much of a realist not to know the truth of that. But what if all that was needed was a spark? A spark to make the rest of the uplands realize they weren't trapped in this life, that they had options. Well then, that could very well fan the flame of true revolution.

"It's all right, Da," Neval murmured, hearing the thickness in his own voice.

Erik turned to his son, eyes blinking blearily. Neval turned to face him, truly meeting his gaze for the first time in what felt like years. When he looked at his father, he no longer felt anger, shame, or guilt. He wouldn't excuse his father's actions, cruel as they had been. But they no longer held such sway over him. There was just . . . this. This moment, this time, this opportunity. And he realized then that forgiveness wasn't given to free his father. It was to free himself.

"You did what you could, Da." Neval whispered the words like a prayer, watching as tears filled his father's eyes. "I know that now. And now it's my turn."

And without another word, Neval pushed himself off the wall and turned toward the village, seeing for the first time the path that lay ahead. He was not a farmer or a drunk like his father. Nor was he an architect, hiding his origins and living as a downlander. He was an uplander through and through. And what his people needed now was not false promises or empty dreams, but a leader.

THIRTEEN

By the time Neval entered the meeting place — Old Joe's tavern at the edge of town — his ears buzzed and his heart thrummed in his chest.

The main room was empty save for an old man asleep in a chair by the fire and Old Joe himself perched behind the bar, filthy rag in hand as he ran it over ceramic mugs. Neval made his way toward him.

"Am I too late then? Has the meeting finished?"

Old Joe snorted, his thick red eyebrows pressing together with little humor.

"Oh, they've been at it for a good half hour, though I'm sure they're just gettin' started." He nodded to the back room, where the low hum of voices crept below the cracked sill along with the warm glow of candlelight. Neval pushed off from the bar, making his way toward the door.

"It's no use, boy," Old Joe called from behind him. "They're all talk in there. Mark my words, nothin' will come of it."

Neval paused. There it was again, that same exhausted defeat that had echoed in his father's voice. Neval felt cold fury bubble up inside his chest.

No more.

He pushed his way through to the back room.

"—not even mid-season and my crops are all but ruined. Sitting in this damn water, they've all gone to rot, haven't they?"

"Well, the stock in my store's all but run through. I can't get new deliveries now, can I? Not with the roads in such a state."

"I reckon the Bellators are in the same state. Or at least they'd better be for the amount of supplies they've *requisitioned* from my farm. I've barely enough feed for me animals, those that still live that is. . ."

The litany continued, men and women, farmers and townsfolk alike. It seemed none had been spared—all worn to the bone. There were no tears, and no real anger, even. Rather, the complaints were uttered with the passive acceptance of their inevitability. And in the eyes of all, the glint of helplessness, fear, and grief shone through.

"They won't stop, will they?" Neval breathed. "No matter what we do, no matter what we say, they will never take their boots off our necks."

Slowly the hum of voices around him faded and all eyes fell on him, but Neval barely noticed, caught as he was in the thrall of a trance. The sensation thrummed in his body, tensing his muscles and coating his voice with a quiver he barely recognized. Looking around, he saw some villagers nodding in agreement, but still more stared skeptically back at him. He knew their doubts, had felt them himself, rolling his eyes as Rowan had railed against the excesses of the Empire.

"We won't be enough," Neval said flatly, registering the surprise on his audience's faces. "We can't be. One upland village against the might of the Empire. I know you see that too. But what choice is there? Leave our home? The land our families have held for generations? The homes you built with your own hands? The fields and shops you toiled away years of your lives in?"

Neval paused, scanning the crowd and seeing their heads nod in agreement. They were with him on this, but would they follow further?

"What's to be done, then?"

A voice called out from the back of the room and Neval turned to see Rowan come to stand beside him, a small smile of encouragement on his lips as he nodded. Neval took a deep breath, strengthened by his friend's show of solidarity.

"A gesture," he said finally. "Something big enough that other villages take notice. Something that emboldens others to rise with us. We must take a stand—take a stand and hope that others follow."

"And if they don't?" The question was shouted from behind them but there was a growing murmur of agreement. Neval swallowed, feeling sweat prickle at his brow, and he hesitated. Who was he to ask these people to risk their lives? After all, look what had happened in their last attempt at thwarting the Empire.

But then he remembered the dead look in his father's eyes, the exhaustion carved into Old Joe's face, and the hopelessness that bent the shoulders of the crowd before him. No, this was the only course that remained to them, the only path that might restore the soul of this place — his home.

"Then we stand alone," Neval declared, making eye contact with each person who stood before him. "Better to meet a swift end than waste away in a land the rest of the world has all but forgotten, dying a slow death over years eaten away by despair and defeat."

Silence fell heavily across the room as the crowd took in his words. Then indistinct murmurs of agreement grew into fervent nods and cries of "hear, hear!"

Neval let out a slow breath and Rowan clapped a hand on his shoulder. "Where, Neval? Where do we strike?"

Neval blinked against a moment of uncertainty, followed by a realization so obvious he was shocked it had never crossed his mind before. Neval stood taller, bringing a fist down hard against a nearby table.

"The dam," he said finally, rewarded by boisterous shouts of agreement. "It has to be the dam—the thing that threatens our very way of life, the thing they've sworn to protect at all costs."

Cheers echoed from around the room, but Neval was still met with some frowns of uncertainty. Neval racked his brain, thinking back to every speech and monologue Tegan had ever read to him. All those lines of poetry committed firmly to memory to spare himself the humiliation of reading in public. Oh, what he'd give for a fraction of those orators' abilities just then. Neval turned then to see Gregor the blacksmith standing with the other craftsman and clapping loudly, offering him a small smile of encouragement.

Then inspiration struck.

"Gregor," Neval called. Gregor's eyes widened in surprise.

"Here lad."

"What are the tools of your trade?"

Gregor blinked in confusion. "Eh—well I 'ave me forge, an anvil, and this 'ere hammer. Belonged to my father. Never steered me wrong, it hasn't."

Neval nodded, as if considering this.

"May I see it?"

Gregor shrugged before heaving his hammer off his belt loop and passing it to Neval.

Neval nodded in thanks, testing the heft of the tool and noting the faint whiff of molten metal and charred wood. He ran a hand along the solid oak handle, worn smooth by the touch of calloused hands over decades.

"This tool is a symbol of your trade, Gregor, the means by which you earn your livelihood—a livelihood that is threatened by the cold steel of the Empire." Neval paused, letting his words settle on the rapt crowd, feeling the thrill of holding their attention creep up his spine. "But you are not bested by any steel, are you Gregor?"

"No lad, I certainly am not," the older man growled, his words met by a roar of approval.

"And neither shall we be." Neval declared. "That precious dam will be the anvil upon which this land is beaten, shaped and remolded into a new world—a better world. A world in which every man and woman alike may live without the fear of losing everything, of having their very lives crushed under Bellatori boots. With this hammer, we will strike the world anew!"

The crowd roared, and men and women alike pressed forward to shake his hand and clap him on the back. Neval grinned back, basking despite himself in the glow of their adoration. All his life, he'd yearned for their acceptance, their approval. And now here he was, all eyes on him, not in anger or hostility, but filled with warmth. Their cheers, embraces, and clasped hands filled a hole he'd rarely admitted he carried but that now seemed undeniable.

He didn't want to think about what might happen should he lose it.

The buzz of feverish delight lasted for only a few minutes before someone shouted from the back of the room.

"But how shall we do it? That dam is already massive!"

Slowly, the crowd's excitement dimmed and a few voices echoed the question.

Jaw clenched, Rowan heaved himself onto the nearest table, motioning for silence as he addressed the crowd himself. "The details will get sorted, don't you worry. Neval and I will head out there tomorrow," Rowan said firmly. "Scout the place out and come up with a plan."

There was a murmuring around the room, as the gathered crowd looked dubiously between the two of them and some glared at Rowan with outright hostility. Neval shifted uneasily under their gaze, trying and failing to discreetly rub his sweating palms against his trouser legs. This was his plan. If it failed —

"Oi!" Rowan barked, silencing everyone with the latent authority in his voice. "I know I've made mistakes, and that good people have suffered a-and died because of them." Rowan's voice broke slightly and Neval's chest ached at the sound of it. "But this time it'll be different. Neval's my best mate. You all know he's brave by now, takin' on two Bellators single-handed like. Yeah, well, I've known him all my life and I can tell you he's also bloody brilliant — not that you lot would've noticed, always going on about his Da, somethin' he couldn't even help." Rowan's narrowed stare circled the room, falling on each face in turn, some hostile but most varying degrees of sheepish. "Nah, you all don't deserve his help, not after how you've treated him. But you know what? He'll help you anyway. Because he's *good* and *honest*, and the best mate a roan could ask for. So if he says he can bring down that bloody dam, well, I for one ain't gonna be the one that stands in his way. Now, who else is with me?"

There was a moment of silence as all eyes settled on Neval—searching, questioning. Neval didn't breathe, didn't dare break the spell that Rowan's words had cast. And then, from the back of the room, a tall burly man with a thick red beard and even thicker brows slowly pushed his way to the front of the room. Old Joe had slipped in at some point and heard everything, it seemed. Old Joe's eyes searched Neval's—seeking, probing. Whatever they saw made him clasp his hand and squeeze it firmly.

"Man of action. Man of honor. Now *that* is someone who can make things happen. I'm with you, lad."

"As am I," Gregor declared, stepping forward, hammer at the ready.

And then there was cheering and Neval found himself once more carried by the swell of approval and excitement. Voice after voice swore their dedication to the cause, offered their services and gave freely their encouragement.

Dazed, Neval looked from face to face before finally settling on Rowan's broad grin. And he couldn't fight the wave of nausea that hit him.

Good and honest . . . Best mate a roan could ask for.

He was none of those things, not in the slightest. He knew it and soon enough Rowan would know it, too. It was time, he decided. No matter what Tegan said, it was time for Rowan to know the truth. He deserved nothing less.

FOURTEEN

I have to tell him.

The thought echoed through his mind throughout their hike out to the dam's construction site. Rowan kept up a constant chatter about strategy and plans for how their act of sabotage might kick off a broader rebellion. Neval smiled and nodded, barely registering Rowan's words.

Guilt gnawed at him with every step that brought them closer to the dam and the danger Neval had all but sentenced them to.

He deserves to know.

Neval swallowed. What Rowan deserved was never in question. No, the real question was *how*. How does one tell their best friend about a betrayal such as this?

We never meant for this to happen . . . Please understand, Rowan . . . Neither of us could have predicted it . . .

Neval groaned audibly as he considered and dismissed each thought. They all sounded far too much like excuses and an excuse was something he would not permit himself—not when his best friend was currently risking his life to follow through on his hair-brained scheme.

"What was that?" Rowan asked, briefly distracted by Neval's groan.

Neval started, "N-nothing. Sorry, you were saying?"

"Only that we'll need something to draw them away, distract

them long enough for us to bring down the dam itself. Any thought about how you're goin' to do that, by the way?" Rowan shot him a glance out of the corner of his eye.

"I've got some ideas," Neval said evasively.

Lies. More lies.

The truth was Neval had lain awake half the night, staring at the ceiling of their shack and wracking his brain for how exactly they were going to do this. The plan had seemed so obvious at the meeting. Buoyed by the excitement of the crowd, going after the dam had seemed the natural next step, the one gesture big enough to get the attention of other upland villages.

In the harsh light of day and without his bubbling anger fueling his courage, the full weight of his actions crashed down upon him, leaving only guilt in their wake — that, and a rising sense of panic that he'd gotten them into a situation that neither of them were likely to make it out of.

He spoke none of this aloud as they headed south along the river, judging their progress by the gradual widening of its banks. It wouldn't be long before all of this land was under water.

The sound of picks on rock and the shouts of men greeted them as they quietly approached the construction site, careful to keep to the foliage of the far bank and out of sight as they creeped around the growing reservoir.

The dam itself was a work of beauty. Even Neval had to admit that. Already taller than two grown men, the rock structure stretched between two cliff faces, blocking the route the river normally cut through the mountainous terrain as it flowed toward the downlands. But this was no normal rock wall and the closer to it they came, the louder the thrum of excitement in Neval's chest grew.

"Incredible," Neval whispered, eyes going wide at the sight of it. "Can it really be . . . I've never seen one in person."

"What's so impressive about it, then?" Rowan muttered. "Just a stone wall from the looks of it, though a bloody big one, to be sure."

Neval shook his head fiercely, gripping Rowan's sleeve as he gestured toward the structure. "See how it curves inward, toward the water? It's forming an arch, using the weight of the water on our side to strengthen rather than weaken it, pushing each stone more solidly in place against its neighbor." Neval made an interweaving motion with his fingers, forcing them together briskly to illustrate his point. "It's the same reason the Bellators build arches into their towers, obviously this time more . . . massive. Pretty ingenious, actually. I wonder what angle they cut the edges at? It seems to me—"

"Yeah yeah. That's all well and good, mate, but what does all that mean for our plan? How do we bring it *down*?"

Neval bit his lower lip and rubbed one hand against the thin stubble of his jaw. To facilitate construction, the Bellators had constructed a small canal that rerouted the worst of the spring rains down the mountain but had relied on hastily constructed bulwarks to keep the bulk of the water at bay. Now that the foundation was built, water could slowly overflow the bulwarks and lap against the base of the dam as it stretched ever higher.

No, taking down this feat of engineering would be a puzzle. But if there was one thing Neval was good at, it was puzzles.

Without another word, Neval set off through the underbrush, ignoring the muttered cursing of Rowan in his wake. He darted in between trees, sliding down the loose till of an embankment until he stood right on the edge of the far side of the western cliff face. From here, the valley south of the dam stretched below him and he could see the entire Bellatori camp and construction site straddling the nearly dried-up river bed.

"Neval, what in Pneumos' name—,"

Rowan barreled out of the brush behind him, nearly sending the two of them tumbling off the edge of the cliff. Neval put up an arm, steadying the two of them just in time.

"See those buttresses down there? The design shouldn't need them. The curve of the wall and the water behind should be enough to keep the structure steady."

Rowan ran his fingers through his hair wearily. "So what, Neval?"

"So the rock hasn't settled yet. It hasn't rained enough to fully compress the rock into the desired shape. Which means the wall is weaker than it looks."

Rowan's brows shot up in sudden interest.

"I see, so what? We take some pick-axes to it one night? Bring the whole thing down?"

Neval shook his head, brow still furrowed as he considered the structure below.

"No, I think we have to tunnel under it."

Rowan's mouth fell open and he gaped. "Tunnel under — are you out of your mind? Why would we do that? We want the bloody thing gone, not—"

"We collapse it from below," Neval murmured, a slow smile creeping over his face.

This could work. This could actually work.

"I still don't underst—"

"It's how the Marians brought down the walls of Port Karthaíla in Old Loren hundreds of years ago. We read about it in Cato Procillius's History of the Empire. A months-long siege came to a sudden end when the walls simply collapsed in on themselves, collapsed into the tunnels that cut beneath them. While all the old windbags on the Council of Benadur were busy bickering amongst themselves, the Marians were hard at work tunneling into oblivion. After all, if there's one thing the Empire does better than anyone, it's building something out of nothing, and quickly. Well, now it's our turn to use their own tricks against them."

Rowan was quiet for a long moment before letting out a low whistle.

Neval grinned broadly back at him, clapping him on the shoulder. "We can do this, Rowan. We can actually do this."

Rowan stared at him, unblinking in the fading light.

"You really think so?"

Neval hesitated, caught off guard, and chuckled nervously.

"What happened to 'I'd follow this bloke to the end?'"

Rowan didn't smile, but merely continued to stare at him.

"I meant what I said, Neval. You're bloody brilliant. Too good for this place, that's for sure. But what you're asking . . . Folk will die, Neval. Even if everythin' goes exactly as planned, not everyone's comin' home. And that feels . . . terrible. Trust me, I should know." Rowan's words were bitter and Neval ached at the pain in his voice.

"Can I trust you, Neval? Not just with my life, but that of our friends, our neighbors?"

Neval swallowed hard, fighting the wave of nausea that threatened to pull him under. It was that word, *trust*, that made him realize the enormity of what he was asking of his best friend. To risk his life, to follow him, Neval, into the unknown and perilous. And the truth burrowed into him like termites, a truth he'd been running from but could no longer hope to escape. No, he couldn't tell Rowan of this ultimate betrayal, which left only one course of action.

He had to end it.

It was Tegan herself who'd once posed the question, back when the three of them had attended school together.

Are there not things more important than love?

Are there not duties and obligations, causes and missions that must always come first? Even at the cost of all you hold dear?

And as Neval stood there staring at his best friend, he knew for once and for all that, as usual, Tegan had been right. There was only one thing to do.

"You can trust me, Rowan. I promise you that."

FIFTEEN

As soon as they reached the village, Neval made his excuses to Rowan and slipped into the night. He took the long way back, slipping in between buildings and weaving through back alleys, well aware that he was recklessly breaking the Bellatori curfew.

The general store appeared around the corner and Neval slipped to the back staircase, which he knew led to the family's home above. He rapped quietly on the solid oak door, praying Tegan would hear the noise first.

He'd never been that lucky.

The door opened a crack and a single green eye stared out at him, narrowing as it recognized him.

"What do you want then, boy?"

Neval's heart sank and he swallowed convulsively. What was it about this woman that a single withering stare could reduce him to a puddle no matter how old he got?

"Evenin' Mrs. Rourke. I wonder, is Tegan home?"

"Of course she is," Flora Rourke snapped. "*My* daughter doesn't go around breaking curfew."

"Then please, might I speak with her? Just for a moment, see."

Tegan's mother eyed him with obvious dislike. There was a reason, after all, that she'd pushed for her daughter's engagement to Rowan, an apprentice, a man with a trade—not a peasant like the one currently perched on her doorstep.

"What for?"

"I've got a message from Rowan," Neval improvised. "He's been held up at the blacksmith's shop all evenin' or else he'd have come himself."

Flora cocked her head and considered him, her expression making it clear she found the friendship between Rowan and Neval confounding, to say the least.

But after a moment, she merely huffed her disapproval, muttering, "Oh very well. Wait here then."

Neval waited, rubbing his hands together against the evening chill as he desperately tried to find the words for what must come next.

And then she was there, freckled nose and all.

"Breaking curfew! Are you mad?" Tegan asked, the scolding tone of her voice softened by the impish grin spreading across her face.

"Look Tegan, I came to—"

Neval's words were cut off as she pushed past him, grabbing his hand as she tugged him down the stairs and around the corner to the woodshed behind the building.

"Tegan wait, I really think . . ."

Neval's words faded in his throat as she spun to face him, face flushed and glowing in the moonlight. Neval swallowed, trying desperately to focus on the reason he'd come.

I have to end it.

Then she kissed him.

His mind instantly went blank as she pushed him back against the woodshed. Her mouth opened slightly as her arms came around his neck, body pressing against the length of him. Neval groaned huskily, before giving in and twisting his fingers in the silken honey waves of her hair. Tegan let out a tiny squeak that he swallowed whole.

He kissed her feverishly, knowing in the back of his mind that this was likely to be their last—one final moment of feeling wholly and completely loved by another person.

With a strangled groan, he pushed her away, holding her at arm's length, as much to brace himself as her.

Tegan chuckled, brushing tangled strands of hair away from her face.

"Good to see you as always, Neval."

Neval smiled thinly before closing his eyes as he tried desperately to get a hold of himself.

"Now what was it you wanted to tell me? Or are we risking my mother's wrath for the fun of it? Not that I'm opposed, mind you—"

"The dam," Neval finally croaked, the chill of the word enough of an icy dousing to cool his inflamed body. "We're going after the dam."

Tegan's eyes widened, her lips parting slightly as she stared back at him, immediately understanding. Then she nodded slowly.

"You'll take care of it," she said. "It's perfect for you."

The quiet confidence she had in him cut him to the core and, for a moment, he rethought his entire plan.

This was *Tegan*.

She had always believed in him, even when no one else thought him worth anything at all. She had seen him, seen his worth, had been his friend. They could leave, he thought wildly. They could make a new life somewhere else far from here. They could be together.

And then he thought of Rowan, who'd vouched for him so bravely. He thought of Old Joe and Gregor, the blacksmith, men well into middle age, yet willing to follow a kid with an impossible plan. They needed him. They needed to *trust* him. And he had to be worthy of that trust.

"It's over Tegan," Neval whispered, holding her gaze in the pale moonlight. "We have to end it."

Tegan's brow furrowed and she cocked her head up at him.

"End what?"

The words caught in his throat, but he somehow got them out all the same.

"We can't be together, Tegan. I'm so sorry."

Her face remained unchanged—the tiny step backwards she took the only sign that she'd heard anything. But Neval felt it, felt the space between them, its icy air cutting deep into his chest.

"What are you talking about?"

Neval sucked in a quick breath.

"We can't keep doing this—the lying, the sneaking around. It isn't right and I can't take it anymore. And Rowan—" Neval caught his breath as he thought about his friend's broad grin.

You're my best mate . . . Of course, I trust you.

"We can't keep doing this to him. It's wrong. He's our *friend* and he deserves better."

Tegan's nostrils flared slightly and her gaze fell to the ground as she chewed savagely on her lower lip.

"Fine," she said finally. "Let's tell him then, if that's what you want. I'd hoped to spare him until all this was sorted but—"

"Tegan," Neval breathed.

She froze at the tone in his voice and stared up at him, eyes narrowed.

"It's over, Tegan. It has to be over between us."

"What are you talking about?"

"The dam, the plan, it's all my idea. Folk are trusting me, risking their lives for this. If they find out all this time I've been —
"

"So let me get this straight," Tegan hissed through her teeth. "You don't want to be with me because you're worried what people will *think*?"

Her words stung, and Neval's teeth clenched as he glared back at her. Before he could think better of it, he spat out, "I should have known you wouldn't understand—you bein' the village *princess*. Never at a loss for suitors, money, or opportunity. You wouldn't know what it's like to be despised, to be told your entire life you were nothing, and then suddenly to be given this one thing—this one opportunity to be better, to be *someone*."

Neval could hear the bitterness in his voice, the sharpness seeming to come from someone else. He glanced up to find Tegan gaping at him, looking like she'd just been slapped.

"*Opportunity*?" she hissed. "Is that what you think I have,

Neval? Is that what you think of the village *princess*? I thought you of all people would understand, would see the truth. I am *nothing* —a piece of meat maybe, something to be owned, sold to the highest bidder with no escape in sight. I'm *trapped* here, Neval, and I just thought — "

Tegan shook her head, her words fading away as she stared up at the moon, unusually bright for so early in the evening.

Neval felt like someone had gut punched him and he reached out a hand to her. She jerked away.

"Tegan, look. I didn't mean—"

"I know exactly what you meant, Neval. You were quite clear. It's over. We're done. Now I think you'd better leave."

Neval stared at her. Tegan didn't cry, though her wide eyes burned glassy as she stared up at him, arms wrapped tightly around her stomach and hands balled into fists.

Every inch of him ached to touch her, to pull her into his arms and never let go. But he didn't. He held himself back and the space between them stretched wide—a chasm neither dared cross.

Finally, Neval swallowed and nodded.

"Goodbye, Tegan."

Tegan said nothing, but her lips pressed tightly together, eyes wet as she jerked a quick nod of her head. She twisted away, as if to keep him from seeing the single tear that rolled down her cheek.

But he saw it.

And the sight burned yet another hole in his chest. He forced himself to turn away, taking in a shaky breath as he forced himself to put one foot in front of the other.

A movement to his right caught his eye and Neval's head jerked up to see a shadow move back behind the corner of the Rourke's shop. Neval froze.

"Who's there?" he called, hearing Tegan's sharp inhale from behind him.

The shadow shifted again.

"Come out then," Neval called, no doubt louder than was wise. But his nerves were gone, emotions too frayed by the fight with Tegan for the caution needed so late after curfew.

"Neval," Tegan whispered. "I don't think—"

He waved her off. He was exhausted, in pain, and wanted nothing more than to be done with the entire business. "You clearly have somethin' to say. Well, we're all ears."

The shadows shifted once more and a tall, broad figure appeared and slowly stepped into the moonlight.

From behind him, Tegan sucked in her breath.

Neval's mouth went dry, every inch of him tensing in a sudden fight-or-flight response. But he held himself still, knowing this was one fight he couldn't run from—not anymore.

"Rowan."

"Rowan, please, you have to understand."

His friend didn't slow his stride, and Neval had to double his pace to keep up. Poor Tegan was practically jogging, tears streaming down her face in earnest as she called after them.

"It was an accident, Rowan. Neval and I — We didn't plan this. It just sort of happened. Just listen, please."

Rowan ignored her, shoving open the heavy door to the black-smith's shop and letting it swing heavily backward, nearly smacking Neval in the face.

Neval caught the door, the force of the impact radiating up his arm. But he didn't care, barely registering the pain. He deserved no less. His eyes remained fixed on his friend's back, watching Rowan's hand shake as he poured himself a heaping mug of ale from a nearby barrel, tossing it down his throat before slamming the mug back on the table with a force that made Tegan jump. Rowan's shoulders heaved, but still he refused to turn and look at them. He poured himself another drink.

Neval could only stare. His chest felt like it was caving in and waves of nausea rolled over him. Beside him, Tegan continued to cry quietly, her hands twisting around each other nervously. In that moment, he barely recognized her, barely recognized himself.

What have we done?

After what seemed an eternity, Rowan turned to face them,

knuckles white as he clutched the table behind him — but whether for support or restraint, Neval couldn't say.

"When," Rowan breathed, nostrils flaring as he looked between the two of them. "When did it start?"

Neval took a shaky breath before straightening and squaring his shoulders. No sense hiding from the truth. It was far too late for that.

"After the attack, after I . . ." Neval let his voice trail off. Images of the Bellator in the alley, blood flowing freely in the street, flashed through his mind. He swallowed and forced his gaze back to Rowan's dead-eyed stare.

"So weeks then."

"We didn't mean for it to happen," Tegan whispered, eyes pleading as she hugged herself tightly. "But we've been friends for so long . . ."

"*We* were friends," Rowan cut in, voice icy. "The three of us. Together. That is until you two . . ." Words seemed to fail him and the three of them settled into heavy silence.

Neval stared at him, trying to glimpse the friend he'd known, always quick to laugh or crack a joke to ease any tension. That friend was gone now and there were no words that could heal this rift.

So instead, Neval let his eyes drift over their surroundings, suddenly realizing who was missing.

"Where's Gregor?" Neval asked. It wasn't like the old blacksmith to leave his forge unattended.

"At the tavern," Rowan barked, eyes narrowing at Neval. "Making arrangements, no doubt, for *your* plan."

Neval felt like he'd been sucker punched, the guilt that washed over him settling like a sticky coat over every inch of him.

"We were going to end it," he whispered, eyes searching Rowan's. "That's why I went to see her. We knew we couldn't continue, not with everything — "

"Not with your friends risking their lives for you?" Rowan's voice was hard, edged with pain and without mercy. "I can't believe I actually vouched for you."

"And you," Rowan said, pushing off from the table and stepping toward them. He shoved a thick finger toward Tegan and she took a step back, eyes going wide.

"Not enough *excitement* in your life, Tegan? Were you just *bored?* You and your Crimson Quill . . . did you finally realize that that's all you are, all you'll ever be? All words with nothing to back them up."

Rowan spat on the ground in front of her and Tegan clapped a hand over her mouth, eyes filling with tears. Rowan's jaw tightened.

"I gave you a ring, promised to love and care for you. And all this time, you were running around playing the . . . acting like, like a WHORE."

Tegan squeezed her eyes shut and Neval's stomach clenched. He shoved Rowan's accusing finger aside and pushed himself between them. He and Rowan were now chest to chest and he glared up at his much larger friend.

"Leave her alone, Rowan." Neval said quietly. "It's both of us you're angry with."

Rowan barked out a shaky laugh and stepped back, shaking his head in disbelief as he looked between the two of them.

"Perfect," he muttered, clenching his jaw. "Just damn perfect."

Neval stared at him, guilt churning in his gut even as he ached for his friend's obvious pain.

"I know you're angry, Rowan."

"Damn right I'm angry," Rowan spat. "I trusted you. You *told* me I could trust you. And all the while, you were running around behind my back with my, my—"

Words failing him, Rowan collapsed back in a chair, downing the rest of the ale before slamming the cup down. He watched as it rattled around on its rim, tipping dangerously but not quite falling.

"You were my friends," Rowan whispered. Rowan's throat bobbed and when he looked up at them, all the anger was gone. Left in its wake were lines of pain and confusion—his eyes filled with utter disbelief. He was like a wounded dog, staring up at the owner who'd kicked it without reason, not understanding how someone they loved could have hurt them so badly. Words failed

Neval as he stared back at his friend. What could possibly heal a wound so deep?

What have I done?

Neval was spared having to respond by a sudden crash through the door to the blacksmith's shop. The three of them started, turning as one to see Gregor barreling through the stoop, wheezing as he leaned against the sill.

"What's happened?" Rowan asked, instantly on his feet and on high alert. Neval, too, stiffened. What more could possibly go wrong on this blasted night?

"Raids," Gregor said between heaving breaths. "The Bellatorio, they're raidin' homes and workplaces of suspected rebels." He nodded toward Rowan. "Quick, we have to get rid of everything incriminating. They can't find nothin' to make a sedition charge stick or we're through—both of us."

Rowan nodded and immediately kneeled to unlock a nearby chest.

"Who's been raided so far?" Neval asked, running through a mental list of everyone he'd started distributing supplies to.

Gregor started, staring at him as if he'd just noticed he was there.

"Neval?" he asked, eyes wide. "Lad, I thought . . ."

His voice trailed off and the look he leveled Neval's way made his blood chill.

"*Who* has been raided, Gregor?" Neval asked again, panic slowly building.

Gregor waited another beat before finally replying.

"You, lad."

CHAPTER

SIXTEEN

"They're headed to your farm now, Neval. Plannin' to ransack the place from what Old Joe overheard from some drunken Bellators at the pub."

Neval's feet were at the door before he'd consciously decided to move. Images of his father caught in a drunken stupor flashed before his mind. Then he paused, glancing back at Tegan, still standing a room's length away from Rowan. He hesitated.

"Tegan, do you . . ."

He hesitated, not sure what he had any right to offer, what she would even accept.

"I'll see she makes it home."

Rowan's voice was gruff, but lacked the anger from a few moments before. Neval's gaze shot between them, hesitating. Rowan seemed to have calmed down considerably, but still . . .

"It's fine, Neval," Tegan murmured, trying for a small smile that died immediately on her lips. "We have some things to discuss, anyway."

Neval took a deep breath, looking between the two of them. Then he nodded and ran out into the darkness, praying he wasn't too late.

～

Neval ran, feet sloshing through the floodwaters of the field he cut through, hoping to bypass the main road and reach the farm before the Bellators did. His feet, soaked through, ached with cold, but he pushed onward. Still, his mind flew far ahead to the little shack and the once empty root cellar, now filled to the brim with the torches and weapons used in the raid on the Bellatori camp. Then to his father, no doubt passed out on the bed, unaware of the danger that was headed his way. If they found him, the old man was as good as dead.

Neval's ragged breathing caught in his throat and he felt for a moment like he was choking. He skidded to a stop, bent over with hands on thighs as he drew icy air into his lungs.

It was too much. Far too much. First Tegan, then Rowan, and now this. Neval felt like he was drowning, being tugged deeper and deeper under a crushing wave that showed no sign of abating.

He straightened, forcing the thought from his mind as he staggered forward. There wasn't time, no time at all to dwell on how his life had completely fallen apart in just a few hours. Instead, he focused all his attention on moving his legs, desperately clinging to the one thing left in his control—he could make it in time. He *would* make it in time.

Neval cut across the nearest field, feeling the mud suck at his feet with each step, the smell of rotting food thick in his nostrils. The shack appeared on the horizon and Neval's stomach dropped to see the flicker of candlelight in the window.

No, no, NO.

He ran harder, not lowering his speed as he crashed through the front door, collapsing in a heap before the hearth. He focused on breathing as his eyes darted around the room — empty. The room was empty.

"Neval?" The voice was quiet but might as well have been shouted in the otherwise silence. Neval jumped to his feet, spinning around to find the source of the threat.

His father sat at the table surrounded by wood peelings, a small knife hovering above the wood block he'd been carving moments before. His eyes were clear in the light from the candle flickering at the window and he looked back at Neval with concern, no sign of anger or disgust. Neval stared at him, a hundred memories flooding through him — memories half-forgotten over years of misery and desperation.

Perched in his father's lap as he told him a story.

His mother hugging them both before filling the table with hot, steaming bowls of food.

His father's warm belly laughs mingling with his mother's high, tinkling chuckle.

Neval stared at his father, not daring to speak lest this mirage disappear through the open window. For somehow, someway, his father had returned to him.

"Neval, what is it, Son?"

"Th-the Bellatorio," Neval croaked out. "They're raiding rebel homes, lookin' for evidence. They'll be here any moment. I—I'm so sorry, Da — " Neval's voice choked off, strangled by the irony of all he suddenly stood to lose.

His father was on his feet in an instant. He strode toward him and, after only a moment's hesitation, placed his hands on both of Neval's shoulders, forcing him to look up at him. Neval did, searching his father's face for the answers he knew he wouldn't find.

"Where are they, Son? Whatever it is you've hidden."

Neval took a shaky breath and nodded toward the root cellar. Erik immediately moved to the corner of the room near the hearth, heaving up the heavy trapdoor in the floor.

He whistled quietly, taking in the glint of swords and axes before slamming the door shut.

"You have been busy, Son."

He hesitated for just a moment before jumping to his feet. He grabbed the ragged rug that lay before the hearth and spread it out over the root cellar door before turning back toward Neval.

"Help me, Neval," his voice was low, urgent, miraculously clear of the booze-soaked slur that so often coated it. "We'll move the table."

Neval could only nod, but immediately helped carry the large table over onto the rug, flinching at the hollow sound it made as one leg skidded over the hidden door.

"We should go," Neval said suddenly, glancing wildly up at his father, who'd moved to take up a place by the window. "If we take off now, we can hide somewhere in the village." His mind flitted to thoughts of Tegan's house, Rowan's blacksmith quarters, and flinched. It wasn't like he exactly had anywhere to go now.

"Or we leave town. Forget the dam, we leave Ceffí behind and—"

His words cut off as his father strode toward him, gripping him tight on each arm.

"It's too late for all that, Neval," he said, not unkindly. "They're already here."

Neval's head jerked toward the open window, where indeed he could hear the clang of metal and rhythmic footsteps of the approaching Bellators.

He'd been too late.

Something inside him crumpled and his vision blurred as he stared up at Erik — at long last, the father he'd lost had been returned to him only for the life he'd known to come to a screeching halt.

Neval had thought he'd be brave when the time came. Well, so much for that. The consequences of his own actions had reduced him to no more than a simpering child.

"Da, I—"

"Shhhh," Erik said, low and gentle. "It's all right, son. Leave it to me. Everything will be fine." Then Erik pulled him against his chest, arms pulling him into a crushing embrace. Neval stiffened, unused to the feel of his father's arms around him. Then he inhaled the faint whisper of pandry smoke and all the memories of a childhood untouched by loss and desperation filled his mind. Tears again stung his eyes and Neval wrapped his arms around his father, burying his face in his chest just as he'd done as a child, content to block out the world with all its harsh realities and cruel machinations.

This is what he'd been looking for all along, he realized. Not acclaim or approval, just this. This one singular moment in his father's embrace.

An insistent banging on the door cut through the air with all the icy dread of an approaching gallows. Neval froze, his breath speeding up as his heart pounded in his chest.

"Open up in the name of the Regio!"

Erik pulled away and moved to the door as Neval tried to force himself to relax. He wildly cast around for something to do with his hands and in desperation shoved them into his pockets.

Erik unlatched the door.

"Can I help you, sir?"

"You have been accused of aiding and abetting rebel activity."

"Accused by wh —"

But his question was cutoff as five large Bellators shoved past him. They were followed in by Centus Gregori, whose nose curled at the sight of their hovel.

"We have been ordered to search your home," the Centus proclaimed. "Now stand aside."

His father motioned toward him and Neval joined him at the window as they searched. For being such a measly shack, the Bellators had their own brand of thoroughness. Neval felt his hands ball into fists as a Bellator ran a staff along the shelves of their cupboard, smashing pottery as he went, while another used a knife to slit their mattress from end to end, littering the ground with straw as he searched the casing.

Neval seethed silently, knowing in his heart their actions had nothing to do with a search and everything to do with punishment.

When a third Bellator upended their table, Neval stopped breathing, surreptitiously wiping his sweaty palms against his trousers.

"Nothing here," the Bellator called, and Centus Gregori strode over to join him.

"I'll be the judge of that."

Then his boot clipped the edge of the rug, emitting a tiny hollow sound.

Neval's stomach dropped, and he glanced at his father to see his eyes close in defeat.

"Now, what do we have here?"

The Centus kicked up the edge of the rug to reveal the door to the root cellar.

Something roared in Neval's ears, muffling the words as the Centus turned back to them, brows raised.

"Seems odd to keep your root cellar so inaccessible. Unless, perhaps, there isn't food stored here?"

He was toying with them and neither deigned him with a response. The Centus's eyes narrowed.

"Open it," he snarled. And the other Bellators rushed to heave open the root cellar doors.

The metal gleamed even in the meager hearth light, illuminating the spark of triumph in Centus Gregori's eyes.

"Well, well, well. Seems we found our rebels after all, boys." The Centus's sneer shifted to a snarl as he ordered, "on your knees."

Neval and his father didn't have time to comply before being shoved roughly to the ground. Neval fixed his eyes on the dirt floor, watching as the Centus's pristinely shone boots came to stand directly in front of him.

"I lost Bellators to your futile attempt at rebellion." He said the words quietly, barely above a whisper, but the menace behind them echoed in the silence. "Good men and women. People with families, who I had to write to and explain that their son or daughter died not fighting enemies of Loren, but their own countrymen who had turned against them. Do you know what it is to lose a child?"

The words were directed at Erik and Neval suddenly felt the cool pressure of steel against his throat. He froze, barely daring to breathe.

"Please," Neval's father whimpered. "Have mercy."

"Mercy?" Centus Gregori scoffed. "Like your son had for my Bellators? No, I think blood demands blood here."

Neval squeezed his eyes shut, feeling a sudden calm settle over his limbs. This was it. His number was finally up and there was no way to outrun what had finally caught up with him.

"The weapons are mine."

Neval's eyes snapped open and he gaped at his father, who stared impassively up at Gregori.

"Yours?" The Centus asked incredulously. "What use could an old man have for weapons? No, rebellion is a young man's game and must be cut off at the root."

The blade pressed harder against Neval's throat and his breath hitched, every muscle in him tensing.

"This is my house. Whatever is here belongs to me and me alone."

The pressure of the blade lightened as the Centus considered, suddenly unsure.

"Wait, n—" Neval tried to stand, but the grip of the Bellators holding him only tightened.

"He's a boy," Erik said, cutting him off with a glare. "Not yet of age. He cannot be held responsible for my actions."

"Hmm," the Centus said, considering. The seconds stretched on even as Neval's pulse pounded in his ears. Finally, with a deep sigh of exasperation, Gregori drawled, "Very well. Take him."

The Centus spun on his heel as the Bellators released Neval and hauled Erik up. They were pushing him out the door before Neval could even scramble to his feet.

"Wait, please!" Neval ran forward, only to be caught under both arms by Bellators waiting just outside. "You can't take him! He's just an old man. He wouldn't hurt anybody!"

Centus Gregori eyed Neval like something disgusting that clung to his boot. "Perhaps he should have thought of that before he stockpiled arms against the Empire. I suggest you remember that, boy."

Neval opened his mouth — to argue, to confess — he honestly couldn't say. But his father turned toward him then, hands already bound, and shook his head.

"Live, Neval." His father rasped. "Live . . . for *her*."

Neval's words caught in his throat at the look his father gave him. Erik stared back, not with accusation or contempt, but with the oddest combination of warning, apology, forgiveness, and something else entirely. Neval could barely recognize it for how long he'd gone without seeing it.

Love.

It was love.

And with that realization, something in Neval crumbled. All he could do was sag against the doorway, watching as the Bellators hauled his father into a wagon along with the weapons pulled from their root cellar. In his head roared a cacophony of anger, desperation, guilt, and pain that raged to the point of numbness.

As they left, a few particularly vindictive Bellators kicked down the dirt barrier that kept the rising waters at bay and a growing rivulet trickled through the house, filling the now-empty root cellar.

Neval staggered out of the shack, feeling the first drops of the coming storm spatter on his forehead. He collapsed to his knees in the muddy waters, barely registering the procession of Bellators that faded into the distance. As his vision blurred with tears, he rocked forward, barely catching himself on outstretched hands. He stared down at the water, watching as if outside his own body as drops of blood fell from his head gash and swirled in the brackish soup, mixing with the mud of the long-forgotten fields.

Mud, blood, and tears — this was all that remained. For an uplander, it was the best they could hope for, the only legacy they were truly entitled to.

How had he forgotten that?

A savage howl ripped from his body—pain, anger, and gut-wrenching guilt all mingling together. But a sudden clap of thunder drowned the sound out. This struck him as funny and Neval started laughing hysterically. As the rain fell in earnest, he cackled into the wind, defiant at the realization that he'd truly lost it all. Everything he'd once cared about had been stripped away. And though the weight of his actions bore down upon him, Neval felt a sudden lightness in the realization that he finally had nothing left to lose.

CHAPTER
SEVENTEEN

The dam had to fall.

It was the only thing left, the only thing that might come close to justifying all the loss — the pain Neval had caused.

Tegan was barely speaking to him. Rowan couldn't even look at him. After his arrest, Neval's father had been immediately removed from the village. The talk around town was that he'd been taken to some sort of prison camp to the south, but no one seemed to know where. After a few days, Neval stopped asking. Still, returning every night to that empty shack seemed the worst sort of torture. So he'd taken to sleeping at Old Joe's tavern, dozing off right on top of his sketches amidst toppling stacks of paper, often waking to a blanket thrown over his shoulders by some kindly villager. Gradually, he noticed others glancing at him sidelong, whispered conversations that halted as soon as he entered the room. He was losing it, they said. And they weren't entirely wrong.

Though word of Tegan and Rowan's broken engagement had spread all over town and speculation run rampant, somehow Neval's name had been kept out of it. He'd expected as much of Tegan, but it was yet another debt of gratitude he owed Rowan — not that his friend was speaking to him.

Neval had lost everything, everyone. And still the dam loomed over him, leering at his failure, tempting his ire. This was all he had left — the plan — and he wouldn't let anything get in his way.

So he threw himself into the work with everything he had. All day he sketched plans — running and rerunning his calculations. And every night he ventured into the dark to join those who still followed him, throwing what little strength he had left behind shovels and pickaxes, every day moving just a few feet closer.

They could only conduct work at night, when the dam's builders and their Bellatori guards were all tucked up in their tents. They'd chosen to start work in a shallow cave already carved into the cliff face and used as a den for some long-gone animal. It was close enough to the dam to provide a direct route for the tunnel entrance, but far enough away from camp to avoid Bellatori notice.

Rowan was there like clockwork every night, but never spared a glance his way. Neval tried to pretend he didn't notice.

Things were moving as fast as he had any right to expect, but still one last problem remained — how to quickly and safely collapse the tunnel when the time came.

It was precisely this problem that he was considering, when Tegan suddenly appeared one afternoon in Old Joe's tavern, basket in hand, loaded no doubt with goods from her parents' store. He'd scarcely seen her since the night of the arrest, but he'd read every one of the Crimson Quill's missives. He watched with a curious mixture of pride and fear as they became bolder, demanding not only an end to the dam's construction but a full withdrawal of Bellatori forces from the uplands and equal rights for its citizenry.

Neval's eyes followed her as she waited for Old Joe to retrieve her payment. Neval dropped his gaze as soon as she turned to glance his way. She too hadn't spoken a word to him since the night of his father's arrest. He expected her to ignore him, to take her money and leave. But to his surprise, she headed his way.

She came and stood before him, hands on her hips as she surveyed the sketches and calculations spread before him. She said nothing and the silence stretched like a gulf between them.

"Tegan," Neval said, clearing his throat. "H-how have you been?"

Tegan raised her brows. "Well, my engagement is officially over and my mother refuses to speak with me. So, I guess you could say as well as could be expected."

Neval didn't know what to say to that and shifted uncomfortably under her narrowed gaze.

"I heard about your father," she finally said, voice low and threaded with sorrow. "I'm so sorry, Neval."

"Thanks," he replied, his voice nearly lost in the shuffle of paper as he brushed at the calculations with feigned interest. He hoped she couldn't see the guilt clogging his throat or the shame creeping through his veins.

"Are you . . ." Tegan trailed off, biting her lip, searching for words that wouldn't deepen the wound.

"Fine," Neval cut in, too quickly. "I'm fine."

She nodded, though her eyes, those deep pools of understanding, told him she saw through the lie. Mercifully, she didn't point it out.

Instead, she leaned in, fingers brushing over the parchment strewn across the table. "You always had a head for numbers," she murmured, voice a soft echo in the cramped space.

"Ha," Neval scoffed, a half-smile tugging at his lips despite the darkness that clung to him. "If not for Ludin's favoritism, you would've been top of our class, Tegan."

A memory flickered between them; Tegan standing defiant before their school master, challenging a blatantly unfair grade. Her cheeks flushed with the fire of injustice as she accused him of being the sexist pig he was. Laughter bubbled up from the pit of Neval's stomach, surprising and warm, like sunlight breaking through storm clouds.

"Remember when I switched your and Rowan's assignments?" he blurted, on impulse.

Tegan's chuckle melded with his, the sound wrapping around them like a cloak. "He praised Rowan's work to the skies, talking about how much he'd improved under his *tutelage*, not even realizing it was mine."

"Proved our point, though, didn't it?" Neval grinned, the tension that had stiffened his shoulders slowly unraveling. They were friends — had been since they stood no higher than the cracked stone walls surrounding the village — before passionate kisses and promises too heavy to bear.

They fell into a companionable silence, simply existing together, their shared past a bridge over the chasm carved by heartache. In Tegan's presence, hope sparked within Neval once more, frail but fierce. Perhaps, once this was all over and the fallout from the broken engagement had faded, they could find a path back to one another. And if he ever got that chance, he'd do better. Be better.

The smile faded from Neval's face as his father's image loomed in his mind's eye — the man who'd swung between cruelty and indifference, whose love came steeped in spirits and shadowed by fists. Yet, in a moment that still felt like a distant dream, Erik had stepped into the path of the Bellators' wrath, shielding his son from the repercussions of his own failed rebellion.

Neval's hands trembled atop the calculations, and he forced the words out, thick with emotion. "He saved me . . . after everything. I just can't understand why."

"Your father," Tegan said quietly, her hand finding his, "he did what he thought was right in the end. Despite a lifetime of mistakes, he protected you when it mattered the most."

Neval nodded, a knot lodged in his throat. Her touch was a balm, a steadying force amid the chaos of guilt and grief.

"Choices," Tegan murmured, thoughtfully. "Your father's choices were his and his alone. Maybe this was his way of breaking free from chains he forged a long time ago."

He glanced up at her, the skepticism in his eyes meeting her gentle certainty. "To do one good thing?" Neval's voice cracked, the idea too grand to fit within the confines of a father who'd spent Neval's formative years drowning himself in mogda or taking out his anger on his only son.

"Maybe." She squeezed his hand. "Maybe to be the father you deserved, even if only for a moment. To believe in *you* if not in himself."

"Believe in me?" Neval scoffed, the sound bitter as winter bark. "Why would anyone? I'm broken, Tegan. A supposed leader who can't even read his own plans without sweating blood."

"Stop." Her voice was soft but firm, a command that drew his eyes back to hers. "It's like I've always told you, Neval. *Your struggles don't define you.* You've got a fire in you. Conviction. Principles." She smiled then, warming the deepest crevices of his heart. "We follow because we believe in your vision, in the world you want to create."

His chest tightened, words lodging thick and heavy. It was too much — her faith, her presence. "Thank you," he whispered, if not fully believing her words, then hopeful that maybe someday he might. He sighed heavily.

"Without collapsing that tunnel, though, we're stuck," he muttered, frustration edging each word.

Tegan frowned, eyes following his to the stack of calculations that just wouldn't add up. After a brief hesitation, she leaned closer, her breath a whisper against his ear. "There might be something that can help," she said, her voice low and urgent.

He looked up, caught in the intensity of her gaze. "What do you mean?"

"My father received a shipment recently. Kur-kona, it's called. Reportedly from the Cross-Sea Lands." Tegan's words tumbled out quickly, like pebbles in a landslide. "It was ordered by some . . . client of his, under strict confidentiality. I only know about it because I settle the books. It should have been delivered to Port Galaén this week, but the flooded roads have held up the courier —"

Her words trailed off even as her eyes glimmered with excitement.

"Kur-kona?" Neval echoed, the term foreign yet somehow laced with promise. "I've never heard of it."

"Yeah, that's kind of the point." Tegan responded wryly, brows raised. "But it's a powder — volatile and powerful." She reached for his hand, squeezing it with a conviction that belied her gentle touch. "I can get some for us. For the tunnel. You were planning on setting fire to the wood pillars bracing the ceiling, right?"

Neval's mouth fell open, once more floored by the speed with which she'd deduced and assessed their plan. He could only nod.

"This will be faster," she said confidently. "Burn it in a confined space and the explosion will cave the tunnel in much faster than fire."

Neval raked over his calculations, rubbing his jaw thoughtfully before glancing up to meet Tegan's confident grin with his own. "That could work."

She scoffed. "Of course it should work. Who do you take me for, Brennan?" She quirked one eyebrow up at him and laughed. Neval stared, marveling at how incredibly beautiful she was. As it was, he had to fight every instinct in his body not to lean over and kiss her silly.

"So, I'll be joining you then." Tegan said confidently. "Once the tunnel's finished, of course."

That was enough to stop Neval cold as he stared at her.

"I don't bloody think so."

"I beg your pardon?"

"Absolutely not."

Tegan looked genuinely surprised by his vehemence, but Neval didn't care. All he could think of was the image of his father being hauled off by Bellators to Pneumos knew where. Except in his mind's eye, it was now Tegan being manhandled, and he was practically shaking at the thought of it.

"I don't remember asking your permission." Tegan said, eyes flashing dangerously.

"I don't care what you remember, you're not gettin' anywhere near that dam."

"You need me," she challenged. "I'm the only one who's actually seen Kur-kona used. You all are as likely to blow your own hands off as anything."

"We'll figure it out," Neval said, eyes narrowing.

Tegan puffed a sharp exhalation, opening and closing her mouth without making a sound—positively irate. If Neval hadn't been so shaken by her plan to recklessly put herself in harm's way, he would have laughed. The expression was so quintessentially Tegan.

Neval was still bracing for a long fight when Tegan let out a slow breath through her teeth, her anger evaporating as quickly as it had come. Left in its wake was an almost mournful resignation.

"I am more than just words, Neval."

That caught him up short, and all he could do was stare at her, at the obvious pain filling her eyes.

"T," he whispered. "Of course you are. What Rowan said . . . you know he didn't mean it."

Tegan winced, and Neval felt it like a pain in his own chest.

"It doesn't matter."

"It does, Tegan." He caught himself before he reached for her hand, but didn't slow his words. "You've done so much for the cause. If you could only see — "

She slammed her basket down on the table, startling him into silence. She squeezed her eyes shut, a muscle working in her jaw as an array of emotions flashed across her face.

"What I see, Neval, is what everyone sees — the spoiled rich girl getting her kicks playing rebel without actually risking anything, that is except the relationship she has with the two most important people in her world."

She opened her eyes to meet his, and in them he saw deep pools of regret.

"You were right, Neval. We should have told him sooner. I—I can see that now. It's just . . . I wasn't ready. For some reason, I couldn't let go of the life I was *supposed* to want. I chose instead to do *nothing,* and so ended up hurting a lot of people in the process."

Neval did reach for her hand then, squeezing it gently until she met his eyes.

"*We* hurt a lot of people, Tegan. This isn't all on you."

She nodded, biting her lip slightly.

"Even so, at the end of the day, Neval, Rowan's right. *Deeds* are what matter. *Deeds,* not words. It's all well and good for me to hide behind a page and a fake name, to talk about justice and honor where no one can call out my own failings." She shook her head, swallowing thickly and blinking furiously against the tears that filled her eyes. "This is my home too, Neval. And I have every right and every obligation to fight for it. Don't try to take that away from me."

Neval had nothing to say to that and so just sat there like a lump as Tegan gathered up her things.

"Either way, I'll get you the Kur-kona," she said finally. "But please think about what I said."

And with a small, sad smile, she left the tavern.

Neval didn't move for a long time, staring unseeing at the plans that could topple empires or crumble to dust. The dam, their hope, their doom, all of it rested on his shoulders. And yet, at that moment, none of it seemed to matter as much as running after the girl who held his heart so firmly in her hands. But he didn't move. There were lives and futures at stake, all depending on him. He couldn't let them down. He wouldn't let *her* down.

Later.

There would be time later to smooth things over with Tegan, to reassure her, to make things right between them. He only hoped he'd stay alive long enough to do so.

EIGHTEEN

Neval stared out at the dam, noting the waves of hatred that rolled off him as if from a distance. He felt oddly detached as he observed the object of so much of his time and attention. Over the past few weeks, its expanse had only continued to grow — the high stone walls a taunting reminder of all they stood to lose. They'd had several long days of rain since blocking the Bellators' diverting canal with fallen trees. Long enough that the waves now lapped at the top of the dam's rocky face, straining against its fetters like some sort of caged animal.

Just like us, Neval thought grimly.

He felt the force of those waves in his soul, roaring for freedom and something that tasted suspiciously like revenge.

Neval pushed the thoughts from his mind and turned back to the task at hand, marveling at the long line of uplanders heaving the last bit of rock from the tunnel.

It was almost time.

Neval made his way down the cliff face to the cave entrance — a barely noticeable fissure obscured by trees and heavy over-growth. The entrance was narrow, barely wide enough for a grown man to slide through, but Neval had the advantage of lanky limbs and weeks spent unable to stomach more than the occasional bread crust and broth. So he had no trouble. Inside, the interior was more spacious and Neval was roundly greeted by the workers with warm claps on the back and more than a few nervous jokes and laughter. Neval acknowledged their greeting but continued on into the tunnel, where the air grew thick with the weight of expectation, the tang of nerves a sickly sharp scent that curled in the back of his nostrils.

It was almost time.

Neval looked around, inhaling deeply through his nose to calm his own nerves as he surveyed their progress. They'd been at it for weeks. The work had been painfully slow going from the start and had only picked up speed after they'd escaped the rocky ground of the cliff face and entered the loamy soil of the riverbank.

But if Neval's calculations were correct (and he prayed to Pneumos they were), they'd finally reached the dam and were digging just a few feet below the surface—beneath the ordered Marian stonework, and the tons of churning water just beyond. Neval swallowed thickly and rubbed his sweating palms against his trousers as he tested the nearest brace.

This was the most dangerous part, he knew. When a wayward pickaxe or an overly aggressive shovel could bring them too close to the surface, bringing the massive weight from above crashing down on them. Just the thought made him blanch. It was because of this that Neval had insisted on solid oak for these last few braces, knowing it would make burning them more difficult when they'd reached the end, but not trusting the lives of so many to the porous timber of the riverbank.

Just then there came a creak of the shifting earth above, silencing the crew. Everyone froze, tensing as they stared up at the streams of dirt that trickled from the earthen ceiling. Neval felt his stomach pitch violently as his fingers tightened reflexively on the brace, as if he might hold up the earth through the strength of his will alone. Soon enough, the trickles of dirt slowed and the crew issued a communal sigh of relief.

Neval pushed his hair back from his sweating forehead as he turned toward the entrance and tried for a measured gait as he slipped out of the tunnel.

He reached the cool night air and inhaled deeply, the

refreshing breeze a cool balm to his frayed nerves. They were *so* close.

"Keep it together, Neval. Just a few more feet."

Neval clenched and unclenched his hands, forcing himself to

—

"Talking to yourself again, Neval? You really should do something about that."

Neval's eyes flew open, and he spun to face the woods, eyes widening at the familiar figure who leaned against a nearby tree. Brows raised over green eyes, she looked almost bored as she surveyed the entrance.

Neval gaped at her. "What are you doing here? How did you even find this place?"

Tegan smiled smugly. "You know you're not *that* hard to follow, Neval. Especially when you're lost in your own thoughts."

Tegan grinned widely and Neval scowled at her, but couldn't muster up true annoyance. Inside, his stomach flip-flopped to have her so near.

Suddenly from the woods behind her came gruff shouts and the clank of boots on rock.

Neval froze and saw the blood drain from Tegan's face.

"Who followed you?" he hissed.

"Me?" she shot back. "I followed *you*, remember?"

Neval had just opened his mouth to respond when a snort of disgust from behind made them both spin on their heels. Rowan stood at the cave entrance, arms crossed and scowling darkly at them. Neval straightened, meeting Rowan's eyes. There was nothing to hide here, not anymore.

"Rowan — " Tegan squeaked.

"They wouldn't be talking so loudly if they followed either of you," he said gruffly, ignoring both of them. "Probably a patrol." A muscle clenched in his jaw as he added, "from the sound of it, they're about to have the lucky break of their careers, though. They can't be far now."

Neval's heart thudded in his chest, and he glared at Rowan's apparently calm demeanor as he surveyed Tegan, something tense and complicated swirling in his eyes. Neval felt like groaning. They did *not* have time for whatever confrontation clearly needed to happen here. Did Rowan not care about all the workers they had here? This could ruin everything!

"Right," Neval said, making some quick mental calculations. "It'll have to be enough, then."

"What will?" Tegan asked, eyes still trained nervously on the woods behind her.

"The tunnel." Neval took a deep breath, steadying his voice before adding, "it's time."

Rowan met his eyes then. "You're sure it's long enough?"

"It'll have to be," Neval muttered, pushing past him. Rowan grabbed his arm, fingers digging into his flesh hard enough to make Neval wince, but he refused to give his former friend the satisfaction.

"Is. It. Long. Enough?" Rowan asked again, voice low and eyes fierce.

Neval stopped and met his eyes before nodding. "It's long enough. Just barely, but enough."

Rowan waited another moment, searching Neval's eyes before nodding. "I'll stay and help then."

Neval blinked at Rowan in surprise, hesitating for only a moment before nodding. "Let's clear out the men first. Then we'll get the fire started." Rowan nodded and ran toward the tunnel. Soon, a stream of men emerged. Neval tried to appear calm as he ushered them away from the site, nodding and thanking them, but unable to ignore the tense, worried faces that slipped away into the night. After what seemed an age, Rowan re-emerged. "That's all of them, then."

Neval took a deep breath.

This was it.

"There's no time." Tegan's voice was quiet but firm and they both turned to look at her. "They'll be here in just a few minutes," she continued. "There's no way the fire moves fast enough to collapse it before then."

Neval thought about the thick oak braces he'd insisted on and swallowed. She was right.

"Luckily for you," Tegan continued, lips curling into an eager smile. "I come bearing gifts."

Tegan pulled a silken black bag from the folds of her cloak, the unmistakable geometric designs of the Cross-Sea Lands embroidered across its sides. Neval's mouth fell open and he stared at Tegan as she stood there triumphantly.

"Is that — "

Tegan nodded, "Kur-kona."

It was smaller than Neval would have expected, and he eyed it wearily. She'd mentioned she could get it in the tavern, but he'd assumed it would take a while. Now that it was here . . .

"Tegan, it's too dangerous. We don't even know how it works."

Neval looked around for Rowan, hoping for some reinforcement, but he'd slipped back into the tunnel, no doubt to ensure it was fully evacuated.

A finger stabbed into Neval's chest, and he turned to find Tegan inches away, eyes narrowed as she glared up at him.

"Listen, Neval," she hissed. "We talked about this. This is my fight just as much as it is yours, maybe more so."

Neval's mind flashed back to that night in the alleyway with the two Bellatori soldiers and winced. But Tegan wasn't done. "My home. My future. I am not just words, Neval, and I'll be damned if I let you or anyone else — " she glanced pointedly toward the cave entrance Rowan had disappeared into, " — force me to the sidelines."

Neval could only stare at her. She was truly ferocious, he thought, as the wind whipped strands of hair across her face, and a vice-like grip contracted around his heart. This wasn't just Tegan, his childhood friend and the girl he loved. This was the Crimson Quill—voice of the uplands and a rebel leader in her own right. She deserved this. Pneumos knew she'd earned it with all he'd put her through. How could he deny her the same vengeance they all sought?

Finally, he nodded, and she grinned victoriously.

"Alright then, let's go."

They made their way to the tunnel, slipping through the

fissure-like entrance to find Rowan gathering the prepared sticks and fire-starting supplies.

"Alright that's definitely everyone. Neval, are you sure you — "

Rowan went bug-eyed at the sight of Tegan trailing behind him. "What in Pneumos's bloody — "

Neval waved him off. "There's no time to explain, Rowan. She brought supplies and we need her help. Now we need you to stand guard at the entrance and signal to us if the guards get closer."

Rowan opened his mouth, a furious retort obviously forthcoming from the set of his brow.

"Please, Rowan," Tegan murmured, reaching out to squeeze his arm. It was a brief gesture, but one that made Neval's insides clench unpleasantly. It did, however, have its intended effect. The retort died on Rowan's lips, and Neval saw a muscle working furiously in his friend's jaw as he stared at Tegan, countless emotions flashing in his eyes. Finally, he nodded, and Tegan smiled widely.

Her relief was short-lived as Rowan roughly shook her off. "Fine," he muttered tersely. "Do whatever you want. What else is new?" He shot Neval a glare that hurt worse than any dagger before turning and stomping toward the cave entrance.

"Rowan —" Tegan started after him, but Neval caught her arm gently.

"There isn't time," he whispered, eying another rivulet of soot that rained down from the ceiling. "After," he insisted. "After this is all over, we'll sort out everything."

Tegan's eyes searched his for a moment and in them he saw trust, gratitude, and something that just might have been love.

Neval swallowed the thick emotion that bubbled to the surface and instead turned to the task at hand. Quickly, he began piling the pre-tied haystacks against each of the wooden posts as Tegan spread a thin trail of Kur-kona between each one. They worked as quickly as they could, but still the seconds ticked by, each reverberating in Neval's mind like a thundering chime.

Finally, they reached the end of the tunnel where work had come to a sudden and unexpected halt—beyond the usual distance where Neval would have insisted a wooden brace be installed. Glancing up, Neval noted the distance but brushed it away. In a few short minutes, it wouldn't matter.

Tegan crouched at the end of the tunnel, consolidated the last of the Kur-kona into the tightly woven cloth sack that hung from a leather cord around her neck, no doubt for safekeeping. She compressed the powder firmly with her hands, tying it off so that the last of the air escaped out the top of the bag.

A rumble from above made them both pause and stare wide-eyed up at the ceiling.

"Hurry, Tegan," Neval whispered. They were so close.

Cautiously, Neval moved back to the nearest post, testing its sturdiness as he had a thousand times before.

A drop landed on Neval's nose, rolling down the length, and then another. Neval froze, and as if in slow motion, turned to stare up in horror at the tunnel ceiling, where cracks slowly spread from the point of contact with the brace.

Drip. Drip. Drip.

"Tegan, we need to go, NOW!"

She turned from the end of the tunnel to look back at him, a quizzical look on her face. Neval took a step toward her and then another before a shower of earth opened up directly above them.

CHAPTER

NINETEEN

Years later, when Neval would think back on those next few seconds, the details often grew muddy. But more than anything, he remembered the echo of Tegan's screams, followed by the force of rock and water pummeling him in the chest. Pain shot through his body as he struck first the wooden post and then the stone wall, where a crushing blow to the back of his head sent stars across his already obscured vision as a wave of nausea coursed through him.

As the black crept in from the edges, only one thought pierced through his mind.

Tegan.

Her face, her smile, her laugh, the annoyed look she shot him when he was being obstinate — these were the things he wanted to remember if this was the end. And her face was the last he remembered before the world went black.

Neval woke with a start, coughing and choking against the water that filled his mouth. He rolled over, vomiting his guts onto the cave floor as his eyes blinked against the dim light. Then, with a start, he remembered exactly where he was.

"Tegan?" he called. Scrambling to his feet, he ignored the screaming in his battered muscles and the throbbing of his head.

"Tegan, where are you?" Panic surged through him as he beheld the far side of the tunnel, now completely caved in. Neval stumbled forward, splashing through the water. His mind raced as he clawed at the rock and shifting soot.

She's ok. She has to be ok.

His mental refrain chanted on, refusing to accept what seemed obvious, all the while ignoring the low groan of shifting earth above him. He didn't care, not even if the earth swallowed him whole right then and there. He just had to find her.

And then he heard it.

"Neval?"

He froze. The voice was faint, and he didn't dare breathe as he strained to make out the faint scratching of digging hands.

Neval launched into a frenzy, clawing once more at the rubble until his nails broke and his fingers bled. The voice had gone quiet, and he could no longer hear scratching in return. Panic flooded his senses, making his vision blur and his ears roar.

No, no, no. Please let her be all right.

Then something broke, and a cascade of dirt rained down around him. Neval hacked against the soot filling his lungs and he heard an answering cough dimly in the distance. When his vision cleared, he stared in horror at the massive twin boulders that stood unearthed before him. Their smooth surface was marred only by a thin sliver of air that gaped between them at about eye level. It was through this gap that Neval could just make out honey-colored curls caked with dirt.

"Tegan!" He cried, pressing his face against the crack.

Her answering smile was weak as she tried to turn toward him.

"Neval," she wheezed. "Seems we got ourselves into another pickle."

"It's alright," he said, more to himself than to her. He was already scanning the boulders, calculating angles and figuring out exactly how he could move them. His heart sank as he realized the boulders themselves were each nearly as tall as he was, and easily five times his weight. All the while, the churning sound of rushing water filled the tunnel.

"How much room do you have on your side?"

"M—my foot. It's stuck, Neval. I—I don't think I can free it." He heard splashing as she heaved against the rocks. "A—and the water, Neval, it's getting higher. I've kept the last of the Kur-kona dry, but I won't be able to much longer."

"Forget the damn powder," Neval growled. "I'm getting you out of there."

But his view of Tegan was already shrinking with every shift of earth that filled in the narrow gap between the boulders.

"There isn't time, Neval." Tegan's voice was soft but there was a firmness in it that sent a chill down Neval's spine.

"Don't say that," he snarled.

There had to be a way. There just had to.

"You have to leave now, Neval."

"Like hell I do."

Maybe if he could carve his way around the boulders. The rocks on the edges seemed smaller. Maybe he could lever them out somehow? But even as he thought up the plan, he knew it wouldn't work. What planks remained were propping up what was left of the tunnel ceiling, and with the rate the water was rising, the tunnel would flood long before it caved in and brought the dam down.

"The water's coming faster, Neval. If you stay, we'll both just drown. This is it, Neval, our one chance to save Ceffí, to save our *home*." Her eyes met his, pleading in the faint lantern light from far behind him. "Let me do this, Neval. Let me choose my own fate. I can be a hero, just this once."

Rage and despair and panic all warred within him. His hands shook as he continued to claw at the stone.

"I. Am. Not. Leaving. You. Do you understand me, Tegan Rourke?"

At that moment, she twisted far enough to slip her narrow wrist through the gap, and Neval seized it. He pressed her hand to his face, even as tears fell freely from his eyes.

"Deeds, not words, remember Neval?"

"Forget that," he snarled. "I love you, T. Doesn't *that* matter? Home means *nothing* if you're not there."

He glimpsed her sad smile before she replied.

"Some things are more important than love."

The words hit him like a punch to the gut.

"Don't do this, T. *Please.*"

"Go, Neval, *Live.* Be the person you were meant to be, far away from here. You deserve to be happy."

Neval's chest tightened, and his eyes burned. He opened his mouth to reply, and in that instant, she yanked her hand from his grasp. Realizing too late, he tried to seize hold, but her fingers slipped through his damp hands, leaving only her braided crimson bracelet behind.

"Tegan!" he cried, slamming his fist against the rock. Ignoring the pain, he pounded against those boulders, filled with fear and desperation, before finally collapsing against them.

"It was supposed to be you and me, T," he choked out through sobs. "You and me against the world."

He could just make out her face through the gap and saw her eyes fill with tears. She bit her lip, as if in regret, and for a brief moment, he thought she might have changed her mind, might have decided that their love, that *they* were worth more than any cause. But then she picked up another stone.

"Always," she whispered, before slamming it firmly into the gap and blocking his view of her forever.

"Tegan!" he cried, clawing once more against the unforgiving stone. But she said nothing. His legs gave out and he sagged into the water, pressing his face against the cool stone. For a long moment, he considered staying, letting the inevitable explosion tear him to shreds. He would welcome the weight of that cursed dam crashing down around him. After all, it was what he deserved. And then two lone voices spoke out from the depths of time and memory.

Live, Neval. Live for me. Live for her.

Neval shook his head. It wasn't worth it. He thought of his mother's lifeless face, his father's grief as the Bellatorio hauled him away. None of this was worth it, worth their sacrifice. *He wasn't worth it.*

But then in the distance he heard a deep voice call, "Neval! Tegan! Are you all right?"

Rowan

Dread sank like a pit in his stomach. He would come looking for them, get caught in the explosion himself.

Not Rowan. Not Rowan, too.

As much as Neval may deserve this end, Rowan certainly didn't. And if Tegan was determined to take the dam down with her, at least he could save Rowan.

So Neval stumbled to his feet, eyes blurring against the onslaught of more tears as he scrambled up and out of the tunnel, every step breaking his heart into a thousand pieces as he willed himself to leave behind the one person he loved most in the world.

He found Rowan near the tunnel entrance, dragging rock away to clear a path that Neval quickly scrambled out of. Staggering to his feet, Neval gripped his friend's shoulder.

"We gotta go, Rowan, NOW."

He didn't wait for Rowan's response before dragging him toward the tunnel's entrance. Rowan stumbled after him, confusion filling his voice as he asked. "Wait, where's T? I thought she went down with you?"

Neval opened his mouth to reply, no idea what excuse he could make, what words might convince his friend to save himself. But then a massive explosion erupted from behind, sending Neval and Rowan flying out the tunnel entrance.

And then there was only blackness.

Neval awoke to the sound of howling.

"Where is she, Neval? Pneumos above, what happened? Where is Tegan?"

The words pierced Neval's skull like iron nails, but with an effort, he forced his eyes open to meet Rowan's frantic expression.

"The tunnel," he croaked, voice rough and waterlogged even to his own muffled ears. He rolled onto hands and knees. "I—it collapsed."

"Yes, Neval, I can see that," Rowan growled. "The patrol made for the dam at the first sound of the cracking. But *where* is Tegan?"

And with those words came the horrible comprehension that had been beating at the back of Neval's mind, a realization too terrible to be acknowledged by his fractured mind. Slowly, Neval's eyes trained on the fissure in the cliffside through which gallons of water now sprayed.

Tegan.

"No," Rowan growled, his eyes following Neval's. "Tell me you sent her out first," he snarled.

Neval opened his mouth to speak, unable to tear his eyes away from the geyser of water as a fissure of another kind carved its way through his chest. He couldn't speak, couldn't breathe, could only stare in horror, willing his mind to deny what his eyes so clearly saw.

"She was trapped," he choked out. "I tried to get her out, Rowan. I swear I did. But she — she knew it was hopeless." He swallowed the tears that once more bubbled to the surface. "She wanted her — her *death* to mean something. She wanted to be sure the dam came down."

"No," Rowan growled, and he barreled forward, splashing through the water that now reached his knees. Neval watched as Rowan tried to force his way through the entrance, past the geyser of water that poured from the narrow cave mouth. The muscles of Rowan's bulking frame strained but there was no use. Neval staggered to his feet, fighting the black that curled at the edges of his vision and the piercing pain in his skull as he took one step and then another forward.

"Rowan," he called, hating the misery that curled in his voice. Despair and denial clung to him even as his ever-logical mind reached the only possible conclusion.

Tegan was gone.

A choked sob emerged from Neval as he slumped against the nearest tree, legs threatening to buckle.

"No," Rowan snarled back at him. "We can reach her, damn it. We just—"

A mighty CRACK echoed through the valley.

Neval's head jerked up just in time to see the sudden sagging in the middle of the dam. A moment of shouts and cries from the Bellatori camp reached them before the first geyser erupted from the dam, quickly followed by a second and then a third. And before Neval could fully process what was happening, a giant rumbling rolled through the earth as the mighty rock walls of the dam collapsed in on themselves. The thrashing water that had lapped at the edges of the walls wasted no time at all. Finally freed from its bonds, the waves poured forth, the churning swells of water frothing and roiling as it consumed all in its path.

The Bellatori camp was gone in an instant, swept away by angry, indiscriminate waves and Neval felt a vicious twinge of pleasure at the sight.

You did it, son, his father's voice whispered in his mind. *You made them pay.*

The very thing he had worked for over so many long weeks had finally come to pass. But the realization brought no relief, no sense of accomplishment. In his soul, there was only emptiness as he stared down at the carnage he had wrought. He turned away — the sight bringing up only nausea and bile to the back of his throat.

He could see Rowan had stopped his frantic attempts to breach the cave and now stood staring down at the ruined dam, his own eyes mirroring the hollowness that Neval felt.

Neval swallowed and looked behind, staggering forward as his eyes registered the slowing of the water that poured from the cave.

All he could think about was her — the first time he'd laid eyes on the girl with the freckles and the honey-colored braids, the wide grin that always greeted him, the tinkling laughter that never failed to pull him from his bitterness and self-loathing.

It had always been her, the single brightest light in his life.

And now she was gone.

Rowan still clawed at the collapsed tunnel entrance,

"Please, Tegan," Rowan begged, voice like jagged glass cutting through the air. "Please don't leave me. I'm sorry. I'm so sorry."

Neval opened his mouth to say something — anything — but only a strangled sound emerged as he felt his chest slowly caving in. Neval stared around in a daze until his eyes fell on the braided crimson bracelet he somehow still clutched in one hand — the last good thing he'd ever given her.

The vice around Neval's chest tightened as he stared at Rowan and the mountain where Tegan now lay entombed. His friends, who should have married, had children, and grown old together.

If not for him, they would have. If not for him, they might have had their happy ending.

Grief and guilt pounded down on him as he struggled to stay standing. Instead, he stared up at the moonlit sky as fat rain drops plopped against his face.

More water, he thought, the cruel irony twisting in his gut. *Exactly what we need to wash it all away.*

He closed his eyes, dragging clear air into his lungs as a heavy numbness crept in from his fingers and toes. It swallowed his aching heart, muffling his internal screams. He was vaguely aware of the shouts echoing through the forest, the pounding of heavy boots that approached.

They had to leave. Now.

The thought somehow pierced the fog of his mind, and he stared down at Rowan, now collapsed in a heap at the tunnel's entrance.

"We have to go," Neval croaked.

His friend said nothing, not even registering his presence.

"Rowan, please. The Bellatorio, they're coming." Neval heard the pleading tone in his voice but didn't care, not one bit. He couldn't lose them both. He just couldn't. Neval reached out to gently grip Rowan's shoulder.

His friend spun on him — bloodshot eyes narrowed.

"Haven't you done enough?" Rowan hissed. "I'm not leaving her, not again."

Neval felt the air punch out of him as he met his friend's

furious gaze. This was his fault. All of it. The dam was gone. But at what cost?

He swallowed, shoving down the waves of self-loathing. He had to focus. There simply wasn't time.

I will not lose them both.

Neval's gaze once more met Rowan's and his hand gripped his friend's arm more firmly.

"Hate me if you like, but I'm getting us out of here. I have to. Sh-she wouldn't want you rotting in some Bellatori prison. You know that."

"Don't you dare tell me what she would have wanted." Rowan snarled. "I knew her. She is — she was m-my . . . " Rowan's words choked off, but Neval could feel him relenting as he slowly dragged Rowan away from the tunnel entrance.

Neval could hear the shouts and pounding of boots growing closer as he and Rowan reached the edge of the forest. But he spared one last look toward the collapsed tunnel, the focus of months of effort. Only now the thin sheen of moonlight settled on it like a sparkling veil. In his memory, he heard Tegan's words reading aloud that silly poem from class.

> *Beneath the silvered moonlight's glow,*
> *Upon dappled skin, life's light lies low.*
> *'Twixt love and death, one champion stands,*
> *Bound by unseen, ethereal bands.*

Neval choked back a sob as he forced himself to turn away, to focus on Rowan and getting him home. He owed him that, owed *her* that. But this was all that was left, all he could do, one foot in front of the other as space and eternity stretched between him and the girl he would always love.

CHAPTER

TWENTY

The journey back to Ceffí passed in a blur as Neval and Rowan stumbled their way through the forest. When Rowan tripped over an exposed tree root, Neval gripped him firmly under the arm to steady him. Rowan shook him off with a snarl, and Neval kept his distance after that.

Shouts and cries drifted toward them as they neared the village. Wordlessly, they exchanged a glance before sprinting to the top of the hill. Cresting the top, Neval gaped in shock at the village below.

The dawn light spilled through the clouds, revealing the streets packed with villagers. Shouting and music filled the air as people ran and danced through the streets. The water level had already dropped several inches, thanks no doubt to the now-swollen riverbanks in the South.

"Suppose you're pretty proud of yourself, now." Rowan's usually warm baritone was hoarse, his words flat and lifeless. "Finally, the hero of the hour."

Neval swallowed, trying to muster some sense of pride or accomplishment, but the joy of his neighbors lay far beyond his grasp.

There was nothing left.

Gone was the yearning that had trailed him every day of his life, that ache in his chest that asked why he couldn't—just once

—feel the same sense of belonging that came so easily to everyone else.

What had he been chasing all this time, if not this?

Slowly they made their way down into the village — met at once by cheers and shouts, warm hands clapping them roundly on the back. Neval nodded and tried to muster a smile in response. No one seemed to notice it was forced, too absorbed in their own songs and chants of downfall to the Empire and the Bellatorio.

At the first sign of a thinning in the crowd, Neval tried to slip away. He had to find Tegan's parents, though even the thought felt like a stone settling deep in his stomach.

They had to know, and he had to be the one to tell them. The general store was on the main street, just a few blocks up. If he cut through a side road, he might avoid —

"Not so fast there, lad."

Neval jerked in surprise, only to be tackled from behind by Gregor the Blacksmith.

"I knew you could do it lad, never doubted for a second!"

Neval struggled to draw breath against the crushing embrace, but squeezed out, "Thanks Gregor, now I really have to — "

"Nonsense lad. Today's a day for celebrating. Time to rejoin your neighbors, now."

Before he knew it, Neval was swallowed by the swelling crowd and a moment later hoisted onto two unfamiliar shoulders to resounding cheers.

Neval gasped, struggling to steady himself as they paraded through the streets.

"I always knew he'd amount to great things," Mrs. Flaugherty declared. "And I'm never wrong about these things, now am I?"

"I always said folk underestimated 'im, I did!"

This was wrong.

Neval knew it in his bones, and every part of him itched to escape, but the force of the crowd carried him along, helpless to resist it.

"Really, I do have to — " The words died in his throat as they rounded the corner and Rourke's General Store came into view.

There, on the front porch, stood a grim-faced Rowan with Mr.

and Mrs. Rourke. And amidst the crowd of cheering revelers, Tegan's parents looked ready to crumble. Her mother's face was buried in her husband's chest, shoulders heaving, and Tegan's father's knuckles were white as they gripped the door frame, as if it alone were all that kept him upright.

A wave of nausea rolled over Neval. He was too late. This wasn't right. They couldn't see him like this. Neval struggled, even kneeing a man carrying him in the ribs. But aside from a low grunt of surprise, no one paid him any mind, too caught up in their own celebration.

As the crowd approached, Rowan and the Rourkes turned to regard the procession silently. Flora Rourke's eyes met Neval's and in them he saw her grief and despair bared for all the world to see. But there was more — a hardness and narrowing of the eyes as she regarded him atop the shoulders of a cheering crowd.

Loathing.

He felt it in his bones and every inch of him seemed to wither in response. He shouldn't be here—didn't deserve to be here. In this crowd, in this village, breathing while Tegan lay cold and lifeless. He deserved none of it.

"Let me off," he shouted. "NOW!" Jerking to the left, he surprised the men carrying him enough that their grips loosened and he kicked off, tumbling in a heap to the muddy ground. Wide eyes and shouts of surprise met him as he shoved his way through the crowd. He ignored their questions, their congratulations, all of it. He had to get out of here right now.

The hammering of his pulse in his ears faded the farther he got from the village, his senses seeming to return one by one to his body. Neval didn't think about where he was heading, didn't pause to contemplate his next steps. He didn't dare think, for there lay madness. He just kept moving.

As he moved, he picked up speed, faster and faster until he was in a dead sprint. Neval had always been fast, could always outrun whatever chased him. Trouble was inevitable, but you could always outrun it.

Before he knew it, Neval stood before his father's shack, the last place in the world he ever expected to seek refuge. He didn't stop to think, pushing his way inside. Yanking open cabinet doors and jerking open drawers, he searched for the one constant that had always existed in his life, the acidic smell of it coating every memory he had in this Pneumos-forsaken place.

There was nothing.

Neval cursed aloud, leaning heavily against the wooden table as his chest heaved. Leave it to his father to deny him the one escape he'd always held no qualms in indulging in himself. Even in his absence, he failed to give his son the one thing he needed.

Guilt sliced through Neval's fog of pain as an image of his father alone in some prison cell filled his mind. He shoved it away, instead collapsing onto the bed. His knees curled into his chest and he squeezed his eyes shut just as he had as a child—as if he could shut out the world. And whether from days spent with little sleep or the sheer exhaustion of the last twenty-four hours, somehow, in Pneumos's infinite mercy, he slipped into a restless sleep.

Neval's dreams were restless — filled with the thud of hoofbeats, the rustle of armor, and fists pounding on doors.

Neval awoke with a start to find the pounding was indeed real. No sooner had he realized this than the door to his shack crashed open and Bellatori guards poured in.

Heaved roughly from his bed, Neval didn't even think to resist. He stayed limp as he was dragged across the floor and tossed into the yard outside.

Neval coughed against the mud that suddenly filled his mouth, the thick scent of sodden earth invading his nostrils. Rough hands hauled him to his knees and, blinking furiously, Millus Gaius Flavius slowly came into view.

His face was all sharp angles and his steel-gray eyes glinted with barely contained fury. Looking around the yard, Neval could see he wasn't alone in the sentiment. Everywhere he looked, Bellatori soldiers looked ready to rip his throat out. A few even bore scrapes and bruises, their eyes still swollen and red.

Did they lose people? Neval wondered absently. *People they cared about? Well, they could join the club.*

"Neval Brennan?"

Neval glanced up to meet Gaius Flavius's cold eyes, but said nothing. He refused to give these filthy red cloaks the satisfaction.

Flavius's eyes narrowed further and he took a deep breath, as if steadying something deep inside him, before shaking his head.

"I warned you, boy. I warned you not to throw your life away on some foolhardy *cause*. It serves nothing and no-one in the end. You should have listened."

Fury welled within Neval and he spat on the ground before the Bellator's boots.

"Where's Centus Gregori then? Not around to do your dirty work any longer?"

Around the circle, Bellators snarled at his insolent response and more than a few stepped forward as if to teach him a lesson. They halted instantly as Flavius held up a hand. The only sign he'd heard Neval's words was a sharpening of his gaze and a muscle working furiously in his jaw.

"He's dead," Flavius said quietly. "Him along with his entire centurium. One hundred men and women with lives and families and futures, gone in a single act of futile defiance."

Neval held Flavius's gaze. He wouldn't pity them. Not now. Not when so many of his neighbors lay dead of preventable disease and poverty or displaced to roam Loren without means or purpose. No, the Marians had brought this on themselves.

"You always fancied yourself a murderer, then? Is that what your dear mother would have wanted for you as a babe? To be the slaughterer of men and women whose only crime was trying to serve something greater than themselves?"

Neval swallowed at Flavius' words and his hand flew reflexively to his pocket, where the ceramic shard of his mother's vase could still be felt through the thick fabric.

"Oy, what's that then!" cried a nearby Bellator, who caught Neval's elbow in a viselike grip. Neval tried to shake him off, but it was no use and the other Bellators held him down as his pockets were forcibly emptied. Flavius only watched, expressionless.

"Here we are," the Bellator crowed triumphantly, holding aloft the shard of pottery. "Seems we have a would-be weapon here, sir."

Neval struggled futilely against the arms that pinned him, eyes widening as the Bellator dropped the shard of pottery into the mud and viciously ground it to dust beneath the heel of his boot.

Gone in an instant.

Neval blinked back the sting of tears that sprung to his eyes before continuing his furious twisting. But the Bellators' viselike grip remained firm as ever.

Flavius watched wordlessly as Neval struggled. Then he nodded toward the wagon.

"Load him up with the others."

His words caught Neval up short as he was hauled toward the waiting wagon.

The others?

Sure enough, Neval's friends and neighbors filled the back of the wagon, battered and bruised, the light of defeat filling their eyes as they sat slumped and bound.

"Wait, stop!" Neval cried, struggling anew against the hands that forced him inexorably toward the wagon. He twisted around, eyes meeting their cool reflection in Gaius Flavius' gaze.

"They didn't do anything! They're innocent! It was me, all me! I'm the one you want."

Flavius regarded him cooly before shaking his head.

"You built that tunnel all by yourself, did you? In just a few weeks? If you expect me to believe that, then I was wrong in my estimation of you, lad."

Despair gripped him as Neval was hauled bodily into the wagon, his wrists and ankles bound like the others. One by one, they met his gaze. There was Gregor the blacksmith, Old Joe the tavern keep, and countless others. Neval searched their faces, praying to Pneumos and whoever else might be listening that he wouldn't find —

There he was.

Neval sucked in a sharp breath as his eyes met Rowan's, slumped against the far corner of the wagon.

"I'm sorry, Rowan." Neval managed as a gag was wrestled into his mouth. "I'm so so—" The taste of mildew laced burlap filled his mouth and Neval nearly gagged. But still he fixed his eyes on Rowan's, begging silently for . . . something. He couldn't have said what he wanted. Understanding? Forgiveness? He knew in his gut that he deserved neither. Even so, he couldn't look away.

His friend met his pleading gaze, then turned his entire body away.

Neval felt himself sag, the weight of the last few days settling firmly on his spine until he felt himself physically bend beneath it. A small, selfish part of him was glad he didn't have to watch Tegan be hauled away with them, that she had, in a way, escaped. She had chosen her own destiny at last, even if it meant he would never see her again.

As for the rest of them, it was all for naught, anyway. All their struggle, every sacrifice, it all meant nothing. Flavius had been right all along. The dam would be rebuilt and another generation would pass before the people of Ceffí found it within themselves to resist once more.

The rocking of the wagon lulled Neval into something between sleep and wakefulness as he stared at the passing scenery. His sense of time slipped away as they rolled through the countryside, headed Pneumos knew where. To a courthouse? Or directly to a prison cell?

He couldn't bring himself to muster the energy it took to care and he contented himself with watching the slowly rolling landscape of the riverlands. It wasn't long before the wagon rolled along through the village, and grim-faced villagers emerged to silently watch its progress—the somber procession a mockery of their earlier jubilance.

Had that truly been less than a day before?

Yet movement to the right caught his eye and Neval's breath hitched as he saw a young girl, no older than ten, lift something high into the air.

Neval blinked.

Yet there it was, unmistakable.

It was a writing quill—white plume was dipped in crimson blood which now dripped into the mud at her feet.

The girl's eyes shone bright and defiant as she held the symbol aloft. Neval had to choke back sobs as all around her, the villagers of Ceffí brandished their own quills of every size and shade, all marred by the same blood.

Something inside of him broke at the sight of them, these villagers — so flawed and so very human, yet somehow made brave by the sacrifice of one girl.

They would keep fighting.

The realization struck him in the depths of his soul. Even if the dam was rebuilt, Bellatori oppression redoubled, and the villagers' homes swallowed by water, it wouldn't matter. The Marians of Loren would one day fall, just like the rest of their empire. Because these people, *his* people, had finally learned to stand tall, to speak out, and not accept their meager lot in life. They wanted more, would *fight* for more, and would not go gently into oblivion.

And for the very first time, Neval felt something like hope. He may have wanted to be that spark, the ember that lit the world ablaze. But this was better. Because his kind, brave, brilliant Tegan — she would never be forgotten.

EPILOGUE

Surprisingly, Neval gradually grew used to the routines of prison. He certainly could have done without the darkness, the damp, and the meager rations, but life here had an odd simplicity to it he clung to like a lifeline.

Neval hadn't seen Rowan in months and had no idea if his friend still lived. He and the other rebels from Ceffí had been sent to different locations, no doubt to quell any possibility of joint action.

Well, they needn't have worried. Neval was finished with all that. No, his days were filled with the mindless monotony of manual labor, his nights spent staring off into the blackness, begging it to swallow him whole. And slowly, day in and day out, he felt the person he had been—Neval Brennan, idiot son of the town drunk and feckless rebel leader, fade inexorably into that darkness. He let it go gladly, content to wrap himself in the cool blanket of anonymity.

Sure, there were some hardened criminals to be found, but most seemed to be petty thieves caught once too often or drunks that offended the wrong lord or lady. He didn't pay such stories much mind. No, he kept to his own business and most left him alone, which is exactly how he preferred it.

That is, until one otherwise ordinary day, six months or so after his arrival. While silently eating his allotted slop from the prison mess, Neval felt the table rattle. Startled, he glanced up to find a strange man perched opposite. He was paler than most, impressive given how the lack of sunlight in the prison had sallowed all their complexions, and his dark, stringy hair was tied back into an orderly queue. He sat with long spindly fingers steepled on the table before him as he considered his dinner companion.

Neval dropped his gaze immediately. He didn't recognize this prisoner, so figured he must be a new arrival. Still, no sense in needlessly antagonizing anyone.

"They call me Lisander," the man declared, voice silky smooth and an octave above the usual. "And what may I call you, friend?"

Neval blinked at him, surprised at the man's sudden familiarity. He hesitated for a moment longer before murmuring, "Neval, Neval Brennan."

Lisander grinned widely and extended a hand, which Neval hesitantly accepted. The man's pale fingers were long and thin and his sharp coal-like eyes seemed to miss nothing as they scanned over Neval's rumpled appearance.

"Well then, Neval Brennan. I must confess, I've actually heard quite a bit about you. You're rather famous around these parts."

Neval blinked in surprise. Famous? Him?

Lisander chuckled lowly. "Yes, the boy who took on the Marian Empire."

Neval snorted. "You forgot, *and got his rear handed to him.*"

Lisander inclined his head in acknowledgement and Neval eyed the courtly gesture with interest. Who *was* this man?

"And you?" he asked. "What landed you here?"

"Oh, this and that," Lisander said. "Seems you can't walk across the street these days without violating some little-known Marian regulation."

Neval chuckled ruefully. Wasn't that the truth?

"But I'm more interested in you," Lisander continued, drumming his long fingers thoughtfully against the knotted planks of the table. "A young boy, barely a man, in a backwards upland village, yet by all accounts, surprisingly intelligent given such humble origins . . ."

Neval felt his cheeks flush with pleasure at the man's words and, without consciously deciding to do so, felt himself leaning closer.

". . . comes up with a plan, brilliantly engineered it seems, to destroy a bulwark of modern Marian engineering, and what's more, it *succeeds*!" A spark shone in Lisander's dark eyes as he considered Neval. "And you wonder why you've become something of a celebrity?"

Neval took a deep breath, pushing away the memories that came flooding back at the man's words.

"*Success* is a relative term, friend." Neval muttered, "as you can see." Neval gestured broadly, including himself and their dank surroundings in one sweep.

"Hmm," Lisander murmured, eyes inscrutable as he surveyed him. "Indeed."

Neval forced his gaze back to the stew before him, still fighting off the waves of anguish he'd fought hard to suppress the last few months. The meaning of the gesture was clear, but apparently Lisander couldn't take a hint.

"See, I have some friends both here . . ." Lisander continued, inclining his head toward a group of men Neval only then realized had been watching them with interest.

". . . and on the outside. Friends who find ourselves equally discontent with the Marian brand of justice and coincidentally in need of someone with your particular . . . skill set."

Neval blinked at him in disbelief, ignoring the blood that rushed to his head, pounding in his ears at the man's words. Neval swallowed, getting control of himself before replying, "I'm through with all that."

Lisander's smile was kind, understanding, but his eyes gleamed brightly, a snake with prey in its sights.

"You're a leader of men, Neval," Lisander murmured, voice edged in steel. "It's in your blood, a part of you that can never be erased. You may not have seen it at first, but you can't deny it now. Don't let that go to waste. Don't let *them* stamp it out of you like some no-good piece of rubbish. You're more than that. You've always been more than that, even if others couldn't see it."

Neval swallowed, trying to shove down the memory of Tegan that the all-too familiar words kindled. Hadn't she told him the same thing?

"They've taken so much from you, Neval—friends, family, even a love?"

Neval's head jerked up at his words and Lisander's smile widened and he reached a hand out, gripping Neval's arm in sympathy.

"What was her name?"

Neval swallowed, trying and failing to hold on to the emotionless shield he'd clung to these many months.

"Tegan," he said finally. "Her name was Tegan."

"Ahh," Lisander said, voice dripping with understanding. "So it is grief that muffles your spirit. I confess I know it well, have trudged those fields many a time myself."

Neval searched Lisander's eyes, looking for some sign that the man truly understood the grief, the shame, and the guilt that swirled within him. And somehow, he thought he just might.

The longer Neval stared into the dark pits of Lisander's eyes, the more he felt the numbness he'd carried for the last few months slipping away. And in its absence, he could feel his fingers and toes, the firmness of the bench beneath him. He felt *alive*.

"*They* did this to you. *They* are the cause of all your suffering. *They* are the ones content to tread on you, crushing you beneath their boots like the vermin they believe you are."

Neval felt himself nodding along, not stopping to ask who this "they" even was. For Lisander's words had struck a chord, and for the first time in months, Neval felt something other than the numbness of grief.

"Don't let your sacrifice go to waste, Neval. Don't let *her* sacrifice be for nothing. Let me help you. Together we can make it through, and someday, we will make them pay."

The spark of anger flared in Lisander's eyes and Neval felt its answer kindling deep within his chest, its slow pulsing flame filling the void that had hollowed out his chest for far too long. Suddenly, he felt the grief and shame recede, melting away from that flame of righteous anger that slowly built, infusing every inch of him with a throbbing, steady heat that chased away the chill of the prison's dank interior.

Lisander's lips curled into a smile as he rolled up one ragged sleeve to reveal the faint imprint of a tree, its fronds curling around the man's bony wrist in a scarlet circlet.

"Long live the tree from which liberty springs."

Neval blinked at the surprisingly poetic words—like something out of The Ballads of Leon. Lisander's smile turned knowing.

"Will you join us, Neval? Red Willow needs you. After all, rebellion is a long and honorable tradition in these uplands," Lisander murmured, then chuckled. "Trust me, I would know."

Neval swallowed, taking in once more their surroundings and the group of men at a nearby table who now grinned widely at them, flashing their own scarlet tattoos in silent affinity. And then Neval found himself nodding, because he realized then that nothing in this life or the next could be worse than this existence. And what if, just maybe, something better loomed on the horizon? In that moment, after everything that he'd been through, he was more than willing to take that chance.

NEVAL'S STORY CONTINUES IN...

Chaos Looming

Build more than you break.
Heal more than you destroy.
But what if chaos can't be tamed?

Book 1 in The Legion of Pneumos series.

Read on for a sneak peek...

CHAOS LOOMING
CHAPTER ONE

In the silence of the moonlit forest, all seemed to be in order. Yet the cord of chaos thrummed beneath, heard only by those who cared to listen.

Keira Altman felt that cord in her bones and let its steady pulse ground her. She breathed in the air, thick with anticipation, as the legionnaires creeped through the underbrush, their footsteps light on the dew-laden leaves of the forest floor. Bringing up the rear, Keira followed suit. Barely daring to breathe, her legs moved double time to keep up with the others' loping strides.

When they'd crested the hill, she finally glanced up, sucking air through her teeth at the sight before her. Even in the dead of night, Marek Larghaen's manor cast a pall over the single-story wattle and daub buildings that gathered at the base of the hill, making up the small fishing village of Abalás. The shadow of the tax collector's extravagance stretched menacingly out over its surroundings.

Keira swallowed, refusing to let the others see the nerves that coiled like a nest of vipers in her belly, the way her traitorous limbs threaten to shake. No, she'd asked to be here, pleaded even. She'd been desperate to join this mission despite her mentor Nazor's protests that she was far too inexperienced. Well here she was, creeping around in the pitch black outside the house of possibly the most dangerous man in the uplands. She'd gotten exactly what she'd wanted. Now if only she could keep from screwing it up.

A hissed warning from the lead legionnaire shocked her out of her reverie. He'd dropped to his knees and was gesturing for them to follow suit. Keira dove for the nearest bush, heart pounding and unsheathed blade at the ready. She didn't dare move, instead listening hard for the source of the delay. A movement to her right caught her eye and she saw Danny motioning toward the manor. She inched around the shrubbery just in time to see a flickering candle disappear from the window.

She glanced at Danny, his pale green eyes just visible over the dark mask that covered his mouth and nose. They tightened in silent question and Keira shook her head. She couldn't imagine why anyone would be awake at this hour. In fact, their entire plan hinged on the element of surprise.

What if the old snake had been warned? The corrupt merchant had enough spies—helpless people indebted to him and willing to do anything to escape his grasp. What if they were walking into a trap? Keira squeezed her eyes shut, forcing her breathing to slow as she focused all her attention on the here and now.

You can do this, she reminded herself. Over a year of endless training and she was as ready as she'd ever be. No, this was her shot—maybe her only chance to be admitted to the rites that year. And if she became a full legionnaire . . . well maybe, just maybe, she'd finally find a way home.

Home.

The thought sent a ripple of excitement down her spine and sparked a flame of yearning deep in her gut. Without consciously thinking, her hand went to the gold locket she always wore around her neck—the one her mother had given her on the last day they'd been together. But that was in a world far away from this one—a world filled with everyday miracles like electricity and refrigeration. It had been over a year since her life had been turned upside down—since she'd lost everything and everyone she cared about. Well, this new world had given her a second chance, and she'd be dammed if she let that happen again. Turns out dying has a way of bringing out your determined side.

Danny's quick head jerk brought her back to reality and she creeped her head around the shrubs to see the two lead legionnaires crouched together, heads bent in whispered consultation. Keira's heart thudded a quick staccato.

Would they turn back? There'd be no shame in that. Even though she'd volunteered for this raid, if it ended in retreat, no one could blame her. Sure the rites would remain just outside her grasp, but so too would the humiliation sure to follow if she failed her first true test.

But before she could think herself in any more circles, the lead legionnaire rose to his feet, motioning them forward once again. They continued their slow progress up the hill, one by one, stepping carefully to avoid the loudest patches of underbrush. Keira watched as the other black-clad figures slipped off in pairs, each going to their assault points. A light brush on her arm brought her attention back to Danny, who nodded toward the cellar door at the rear of the lodge. Reminded of their assignment, Keira took a deep breath, steeling herself for the task ahead.

Come on, Altman, don't screw this up.

They reached the cellar doors all too soon and Keira glanced around nervously, scanning for guards who might come to investigate their activities. Danny tried the door handle gingerly, then more forcefully. As they'd guessed, it was latched from the other side. He turned to her expectantly.

Time for Plan B.

Keira wiped her sweaty palms on her trousers, fiddling with the mask that covered her face as her eyes darted around the clearing. Danny's brow furrowed.

"You all right?" He asked, the Boston Irish lilt of his voice barely above a whisper.

Keira nodded, not trusting her voice to come out any stronger than a squeak—not exactly the tone of confidence she'd hoped to convey.

She forced her leaden legs to move as she kneeled before the cellar door. A warm squeeze on her shoulder made her glance up to meet Danny's warm gaze. He gave her a small nod and she felt something warm and gooey fill her insides, filling and soothing the gouges her fear had carved into her in the way only Danny could. There was a reason he was her grounder after all.

She could do this.

She took a deep breath and turned back to the cellar door, feeling Danny move into position to guard her back. She'd be royally screwed if someone tried to sneak up on her once she began the binding process—not the way she hoped to end the night, or her short second life.

Reaching deep inside herself, Keira gently nudged the mass of energy that lay just behind her stomach. Sending it downward through her feet, she firmly anchored herself to the grassy patch she'd chosen. Then, reaching out for the latch, she let the energy flow through her fingers as her lips puckered in a whistle. Called pneuma, or "breath," she knew the energy was too high for normal ears to detect. She felt this energy being twisted and shaped to match the waves of sound, and she altered the pitch of her note, letting it guide the pneuma into the shape she needed— wrought iron. All materials, and even people, had a shape to their pneuma, an amplitude and frequency to the energy holding them together. While a person's pneuma could change over time, the pneuma of objects like this lock remained a constant, unalterable touchstone.

She willed her pneuma to first match the iron's, then alter slightly, slowly disrupting its tidy molecular structure. The latch felt cold in her hand as it pulled the heat from her body, disordering the molecules that comprised it until the metal was nothing more than a molten blob. Wiping the sweat from her brow, Keira grasped the ledge of the door, easing it upward until the metal bindings gave way with a dull *thunk*. Below them stretched earthen steps that led down into the cellar.

Danny began descending the stairs, longsword at the ready. They'd decided he'd go in first, to stall for time should they encounter anyone, and to give her the space to orchestrate a binding if needed. Following close behind, Keira nearly ran smack into Danny, as he he froze at the bottom of the steps. She halted, listening for the sound that had caught his attention.

Bringing a finger to his lips, Danny inched forward again,

deeper into the dank caverns of the cellar. Keira gripped the hilt of her sword and balled her left hand into a fist to hide its shaking.

You can do this. Just keep moving forward.

They were almost to the far end of the cellar now, and Keira could just make out the outline of the promised ladder leading to the main floor above. She barely registered the creak of a door hinge before something slammed her against the wall, sending her sword flying. She dropped to the ground, breath ragged as she tried to keep from heaving onto the floor.

She shoved aside what looked like a chair and scrambled to her feet. Hearing Danny cursing nearby, and the clang of metal as he fought off his own seemingly more human assailant, she staggered forward.

Keira emerged into a filthy larder to see him locked hilt to hilt with one of the conniving Marek Larghaen's hired men. She swore under her breath. They'd hoped to catch him unawares, but it seemed the old bastard had been warned, and had upped his guard to prepare for their arrival.

Keira sprinted toward Danny, shouting his name. His gaze shot up and with a great *umph,* spun the man he'd been grappling with in her direction just as she reached them. She met his back with her blade and felt an unsettling *crunch* as it slid through him. The man slumped against her, and she briefly bore his weight before letting him slide to the ground. He gurgled blood as Keira pulled her sword from his back, then was still.

"You okay?" Danny asked, quickly scanning her up and down.

Keira nodded. She couldn't seem to look away from the man at her feet. He was definitely dead—his eyes had that blank, dilated look that corpses get and he smelled like he'd wet himself. Her mentor, Elliott, had told her the end wasn't pretty, but until this moment, she hadn't fully grasped the horror that would be her first kill. She swallowed hard, avoiding Danny's eyes. She wasn't ready for the understanding and sympathy she knew she'd find there.

Blinking furiously, Keira forced her gaze away from the body. "Fine," she muttered. "You?"

"I'll live."

She knew he wanted to say more, knew the moment he thought better of it. She was grateful for that—Danny always seemed to know exactly what she needed.

"We should keep moving," Danny said. "On account of it seems like the others have run into trouble too. We need to get to Marek before he pulls off another of his grand escapes."

Keira nodded, noticing for the first time the sounds of fighting echoing from elsewhere in the lodge. She wadded up her confusing mix of emotions and flung them to the back of her mind. She'd have time to deal with them later. Peering around for an exit, Keira noted that the larder had seen better days. A thick layer of dust and grease covered the chopping tables and cabinetry, but the still-smoldering embers in the grand fireplace betrayed the room's recent use.

Shouts and curses echoed from the front rooms, but Keira and Danny instead headed for the servants' staircase in the back of the larder. The steps creaked as they swiftly climbed, making for the bedchambers on the floor above. But when an echoing creak reached their ears, they both froze. Any sound was amplified in the tight quarters and Keira barely dared to breathe as the creaking grew closer and closer. Her eyes darted to Danny's to find he'd pressed himself against the far wall, one finger pressed to his lips. Keira similarly eased herself flat against the wall opposite and forced air through her nostrils. *Inhale.* The creaking was just around the corner now. *Exhale.* Keira and Danny leaped forward, swords at the ready.

Tiny squeals and muffled sobs met them as a woman dressed only in a sleeping shift pressed two small children to her.

"Please, oh please," the woman cried. "They're just children. A-and I'm their nursemaid."

Danny was the first to step forward, brandishing a torch from the wall as he quickly surveyed the woman. Her dress was plain enough and she didn't appear to be hiding any weapons, making her story seem plausible.

"What do you think, Keira?" Danny asked. "I wasn't aware Marek had any kids, personally."

Keira didn't answer, throat working silently as her eyes fixed on the two small children. The smallest was a boy, no more than two or three whose sandy brown hair stuck up at odd ends. Fat crocodile tears filled his eyes as he stared up at her and he quickly buried his face in his nursemaid's skirts. But his sister, only a few years older from the looks of it didn't cry but stared wide-eyed at Keira as if transfixed. Her blonde hair was neatly parted with braids framing her face on either side. *Just like Molly.*

"We should see them out," Keira said suddenly. She didn't know where the impulse came from, but once uttered it just felt *right*. She couldn't leave them.

"There isn't time." Danny hissed. "They'll be fine."

But she shook her head and thought about the man and dog they'd encountered in the cellar. There could be more. Staring at the wide-eyed children all she could see was Molly, the little sister who wasn't even truly related to her, and the car accident that meant she may never see her again. But this little girl was here, now, and she'd be damned if she let anything happen to her.

"There could be fighting outside," she whispered back at him. "I have to make sure they make it safely."

"The mission—"

"I'll catch up to you," Keira insisted, sliding one hand into the girl's trembling one as she led the three of them down the steps.

From behind, she heard Danny's whispered curse. But there was no time to worry about that. They were innocent, these three, caught up in something they likely could never understand. She'd been there, silently begging for help from strangers who merely averted their gaze from the uncomfortable or inconvenient. She would never be that person.

It took only a few minutes to see the children and their nursemaid safely out through the cellar—their path thankfully absent any unexpected encounters. When Keira returned to take the stairs two at a time, she nearly ran smack into Danny and swore in surprise.

"Y-you stayed." *Obviously*, she chided herself.

Danny steadied her with one hand, meeting her gaze with a single cocked eyebrow.

"Now when've I eva' left you behind?"

Keira flushed and could only offer a half-hearted shrug. He was right, of course. Danny was nothing if not steadfast and loyal to a fault. He'd sooner have chewed off his own arm than left her back unguarded. It was the thing she loved most about him.

That thought sent a warm tingly sensation all the way to her toes and Keira felt her blush deepen. Now was *definitely* not the time for such thinking.

Luckily Danny had already turned and continued their ascent up the back staircase. Keira hurried after him, hand tightening on the hilt of her sword as she forced herself to refocus. They paused when they reached the landing, and Keira motioned toward a room on their left, where candlelight flickered beneath the closed door. Someone was definitely inside.

They flanked the door, one on either side, and Danny raised his eyebrows at her expectantly. She closed her eyes and concentrated on the pneuma. Slowly, Keira cast it out on the back of an inaudible whistle, searching with her mind for the presence they sought. The pneuma she encountered was twisted, dark, and calculating, but tinged with something else—a nervous tension of sorts. It was definitely Marek, all right, but he wasn't alone.

She could feel him pacing on the other side of the door along with two others, most likely bodyguards. Coming back to herself, she caught Danny's eye and held up three fingers. His brow furrowed. They'd been told Marek had only one bodyguard he trusted to share a room with him as he slept, and the original plan had been for her to muscle bind Marek while Danny took care of the bodyguard. Two guards threw that notion out the window, as she could only cast one bind at a time, and the out-of-body requirements of casting made her useless in a physical fight. That's why Danny was there—to guard her back during the process, and to help bring her back if she lost control. This would be difficult for him to do while fighting off two assailants at once.

She shook her head, and he nodded in response. Though the mask covered half his face, she knew he was grimacing underneath. They'd have to do this the old-fashioned way.

Danny grasped the door's handle while Keira mimed the general location of each of the three targets. Her fingers counted them down. *Three...*her grip tightened on the hilt of her sword... *two...*Danny's calm, determined eyes met hers...*one!*

With a shove, Danny flung open the door and rushed the closest bodyguard. Quick on his heels, Keira sprinted into the room and slammed into the other, meeting his sword with the clang of her own. She cursed their rotten luck—of course they had their weapons at the ready. No doubt they could hear the shouts echoing from the rest of the house.

She didn't have time to think about this long before she felt her sword drawn up and around in a giant arc, disentangling their blades and putting her immediately on the defensive. She barely blocked a crushing overhead swing. *This must be Rhondor*, she thought. *Marek's favorite.* Panic welled within her. *He's too big.*

She quickly squashed the panicked thought and forced herself to think rationally. *This is what you've trained for.* The man was enormous, and the broadsword he wielded nearly doubled his arm's reach. She needed to get some distance, or he'd skewer her for sure. After parrying his next slash, Keira snatched up a ceramic plate from the table behind her. When Rhondor advanced again, she blocked his stroke while simultaneously shattering the plate against his head. He stumbled backward, allowing her a few precious seconds to regain her bearings.

From the corner of her eye, she saw a huddled figure creep along the edge of the room, making for the open hall door.

Oh, no you don't, she thought.

Shifting her sword into her left hand, using the other to snatch up her hip dagger and sent it flying end over end into Marek's side. The man cried out and doubled over in pain.

Keira grinned in satisfaction. *That'll keep him from getting too far.*

Before she could revel in her minor victory, Rhondor was on her again, and he was angrier than ever. Keira, remembering everything her mentor Nazor had ever taught her, spun out of his way, letting his momentum carry him into the wall behind. As she turned, she brought her blade down in a sweeping arc, slicing the giant man collar to navel. It wasn't a deep cut—certainly not mortal—but it was enough to slow his movements as he forced her back on the defensive, hammering her with slashes and stabs. He was tiring, but so was Keira. Her breathing was shallow, and her sword felt heavier with every block.

Rhondor's wound was bleeding freely now, forming a small pool at his feet. Sensing an opportunity, Keira retreated slightly. Rhondor immediately pressed his advantage and leaped toward her, his foot slipping on his own blood. He didn't fall, but he definitely stumbled.

That was all Keira needed.

She lunged forward, cutting a single stroke in and up, wedging her blade between the giant's ribs. He exhaled sharply, then dropped to his knees, blood bubbling past his lips. She let him sag to the floor, then wrenched her blade free and spun to look for Danny.

He was in the opposite corner of the room, dealing the final blow to the other guard, a savage slice to the man's neck that left him in a gurgling heap. Danny turned toward her, and she saw a cruel cut down the side of his left arm. She started forward, brows knit with concern, but he waved her off.

"Just a scratch," Danny reassured her.

She nodded, not entirely convinced, but knew better than to argue just then.

"Where's Marek?" Danny asked.

Keira glanced around and cursed. "Well, he can't have gone far, not with my knife sticking out of his gut."

She saw a ghost of a smile cross Danny's face as he ran for the door. Out in the hallway, he bent to look at something on the floor before motioning her closer.

"Definitely blood. Seems you're not quite as hopeless at knife-throwing as Nazor says," he teased.

Keira scowled. "I told you I hit him. Honestly, I'm surprised he made it this far. From what they told us, I didn't take him for much of a fighter. His type always seems to have others around for the dirty work."

Danny's smile twisted darkly. "Never underestimate the survival instincts of a man like Marek. He didn't get to where he's at for lack of determination."

Keira nodded, gritting her teeth. She'd never met Marek Larghaen, but she knew enough about the snake to suspect that Danny was probably right. The slimy merchant had clambered over the backs of his fellow uplanders to become the local Tiarna's chief tax collector, keeping his power through threats, intimidation, and outright violence. *Yes,* Keira thought grimly, *he was certainly motivated, but that makes two of us.*

A clatter of metal hitting the floor brought their attention to a room at the far end of the hall. The two of them slipped down the hall toward the sound, careful to check each room they passed to ensure they wouldn't be ambushed. As they approached the far door, Keira heard voices coming from inside—laughing, it sounded like. Danny pressed his ear to the door, a puzzled look on his face, then sighed in relief.

Throwing open the door, he and Keira entered to find a cowering Marek, surrounded by four of their fellow Legionnaires. Though masks obscured their faces, Keira quickly recognized their mentors, Elliott and Nazor.

"Nice of you both to join us," Nazor growled.

⁓

The story continues in *Chaos Looming,* in stores now!

GRAB YOUR FREE EXCLUSIVE SHORT STORY!

Dive into Danny's first moments in Loren—meeting Nazor and discovering the unsettling signs of chaos descending on Loren. **FREE for newsletter subscribers!**

Ready to see Loren through Danny's eyes?
Click here to join and claim The Grounder!
www.hbreneau.com/thegrounder

THE BALLADS OF LEON

TRANSLATED BY
CATO PROCILLIUS

My heart, my she-lion, fierce and bold,
Binder of spirits, summoner of old.
Thy voice, it breaks the stones with ease,
Thy might, the terror of our enemies.

∼

Our love, a blaze too fierce to tame,
A river wild no banks can claim.
A tempest that in fury spins,
A sun that burns, a moon that grins.

∼

In the ruins of my kingdom, stand I alone,
My empire fallen, my power flown.
From ashes and sorrow, my spirit calls,
Through shattered dreams and crumbled walls.

~

Beneath the silvered moonlight's glow,
Upon dappled skin, life's light lies low.
'Twixt love and death, one champion stands,
Bound by unseen, ethereal bands.

~

In shadows' hold, old whispers stir,
Ancient melodies, a haunting blur.
Thine eyes once danced with starry light,
Now shut in death's eternal night.

~

Hearts entwined like ivy grows,
Cleft apart by time's cruel blows.
Where thou once stood, naught but a shade,
In silence, I hear the call thou made.

~

From sorrow's deep, a force awakes,
From tears and prayers, its strength it takes.
Though shadows claim thy wandering soul,
Our love shall light both path and toll.

AUTHOR'S NOTE

This book wouldn't have been possible without the help and input of family, friends, classmates, editors, and beta readers.

Special thanks go to my beta readers Mary R. Lanni, Nicole McCarthy, Yar Gul, Jess Bogdan, Elisabeth Allen, Paola Llerenas, and others who shall go unnamed but not unappreciated! Your early feedback and suggestions were absolutely essential to the writing and editing process. Thank you also to Natalia Junqueira for her gorgeous cover design. You did it again!

This was a really tough book for me to write. Not the least of which because I started medical residency in the middle of it. Well, two years later and we finally made it! Somehow amidst the long hours in the ER and too short nights spent in cramped resident call rooms, the story of an unlikely upland rebel refused to leave me alone.

We live in a dark world, the effects of which all too often show up at the Emergency Room's front door. Some days, it's far too easy to feel like our efforts are just a small drop in a sea of untended pain and suffering. So maybe that was why I kept coming back to Neval's story. It's a tale about a young man growing up in desperate times and the bleakest of environments. Despised by his community, he wants nothing more than to change his world, and in so doing, ultimately changes himself.

> *"You write in order to change the world, knowing perfectly well that you probably can't, but also knowing that literature is indispensable to the world. The world changes according to the way people see it, and if you alter, even by a millimeter, the way people look at reality, then you can change it."*
>
> — *JAMES BALDWIN*

Thank you, reader, for your patience and understanding through this dry spell. I promise I've been hard at work behind the scenes and I'm excited to share with you all that I've been working on! Thank you for bearing with me on this crazy journey and I hope his story means as much to you as it has to me!

ABOUT THE AUTHOR

H.B. Reneau is an author of YA and adult fantasy. Author, physician, and proud dog mom, she is known for her character-driven, genre-crossing fiction that draws on her experiences in both emergency medicine and the military. She has a particular love for strong female characters who face up to adversity and manage to subvert some expectations along the way.

To learn more, head over to her website at www.hbre neau.com. There you'll find her books, blog, and fun extras. Or reach out directly! Follow on social media and sign up for the monthly newsletter to receive receive free gifts, awesome discounts, and updates on all her latest projects.

If you enjoyed this book, please consider leaving a review at your favorite online storefront!

ALSO BY H.B. RENEAU

<u>The Legion of Pneumos</u>

Chaos Looming

Haven Enduring

<u>The Legion of Pneumos: Novella Collection</u>

The Cantor

The Centus

The Rebel

The Remnant

www.ingramcontent.com/pod-product-compliance
Lightning Source LLC
Chambersburg PA
CBHW021712190726

48289CB00008B/2497